The Widow Makers

Buck Edwards

For:

Jennifer Moorman
author, editor, and friend

Chapter 1

Yᴇʟᴇɴᴀ ᴡᴀs ᴛʜᴇ ꜰɪʀsᴛ to see the riders, making a tempest of dust across the field and heading her way. She was standing on the hill where the newest of the vegetable gardens had been plotted. She was erecting poles to mark out the boundaries, tapping down the stakes with a flat hammer, little Hazel at her side, holding the ball of twine to be used for lining the perimeter.

The riders were coming from the south, and she turned that way, counting. There were six of them, riding in tight formation, straight on, like some kind of cavalry charge. Yelena threw an urgent glance down into the yard where the big house stood amongst the cottonwoods. Rose of Sharon was down there, her long brown hair across her shoulders, her arms around the neck of a goose, wrestling it to the ground. It was destined for the soup pot if Rose could win the fight.

The horsemen drew nearer, thundering like the men of Armageddon. Hazel saw them too now and she stiffened. Her blonde hair, like Yelena's, was tied onto the top of her head with a sturdy coil of brown ribbon. Yelena drew the eleven-year-old Hazel into the shelter of her arms, and they watched, feeling a cold dread in the way this small army pushed their horses over the last hill and into the yard, their dust following them.

Hazel looked up into Yelena's face, but the older girl simply shook her head, indicating silence.

The horsemen pounded to a stop in the yard, their mounts tramping the hard-packed ground in front of the lawn and the worn path to the big house. Rose of Sharon, in her alarm, had released her hold on the goose's neck, and it honked away, wings flapping its disgust. Rose stood then, shielding her eyes, as the dust drifted across her face and up the hill toward the stable. When she finally looked up at the men, her face showed a glint of steel. She was thirty-five, the oldest, next to Hester, and she saw it as her duty to shepherd the other girls, all thirteen of them.

1

The horsemen wasted no time in stating their business. A tall man wearing a long, black, rider's duster took off his hat and bowed a greeting. Then turning to one of his henchmen, he nodded, and the other man pulled a revolver from its holster and fired a deafening shot into the air. A flurry of birds exploded from the trees and flew in all directions.

The tall man spoke. "Mr. Smoot. You and Lampy clean out that stable. I want the best horses." The two riders, both older with gray whiskers and wiry frames, turned their mounts up the slope to the stable. Then the tall man spoke to Rose of Sharon directly. "Where is your husband? Or your father. Or whatever he is."

Rose gave him an empty stare.

The tall man smiled contemptuously. "I know who you are," he said. "I know who all of you are. You are the wives and children of Bishop Elgin Prescott. Besides a fine herd of lovely wives, he is also the husbandman to some of the best horseflesh in the all of Utah."

Rose of Sharon finally spoke. "What do you want?"

The other riders giggled.

"Ma'am. Please excuse my companions. They are a beastly bunch. I am forever having to check their lack of manners."

"What do you want?" Rose asked again, sternly.

The tall man, still holding his wide brimmed hat, put his fingers through his sandy hair, and then returned the hat to his head. "Where is Bishop Prescott? We need to get this thing rolling."

Rose glanced up the hill and saw Yelena and Hazel standing stiff as scarecrows in the new garden plot. The tall man followed her eyes and then ordered Rose to motion them down into the yard.

"Why?" Rose said.

"Ma'am, you're wearing on me. Get those two girls down here. Now. In fact, I want everyone out here. I want everybody lined up right here in front of me. Line them up like little tin soldiers. Do it now." His voice rose into a testy tone, the *do it now*

2

coming out nearly as a shriek.

Rose motioned for Yelena to bring Hazel down to the yard, and then she walked to a post in the center of the lawn. She pulled a short rope, causing a bronze bell that was attached there to ring. She let the bell ring a dozen times, pulling on the rope with an angry zeal. As it rang more girls and grown women began emerging from the house, some wrapped in aprons, hands powdered with flour; others, young as five or six, unfolded from the corner of the house or from behind trees.

The other three horsemen had not moved. They sat in their saddles, awaiting orders. It took five long minutes to gather everybody and stand them in a line before the tall man. There were a good many of them: tall, short; boys and girls; women. They all stood in stupid confusion, looking at the tall man on his horse, wondering what he wanted with all of them.

Mr. Smoot rode out of the stable herding two boys stumbling in front of him. They wore straw hats and heavy boots, and they clomped down toward the rest of the group in the yard, their youthful eyes flaming red with fear and fighting rage. One of them showed a fresh welt across his face.

Mr. Smoot spoke. "There's as many fine horses as a man could want up there. Lampy's holding 'em."

The tall man nodded his approval and then turned his attention to the line of humanity in front of him. He let out a long breath. "I am Erastus Kammers. I am here to set you free. Rejoice. Today is emancipation day for you."

The group blinked in united bewilderment.

Kammers let his gaze travel down the faces. He stopped at the girl who had come from the hill. "What is your name?"

There was a moment of hesitation before a sturdy voice said, "Yelena."

"Yelena," Kammers repeated. "I like that name. Please stand over there to the side." Yelena glanced at Rose of Sharon and receiving a nod, stepped away from the others.

Kammers' eyes skipped over several others and then stopped

3

at another young woman. "And who are you?"

Elise's shoulders shook, but she told him her name.

"How old are you, girl?"

"I...I am twenty."

"Fine. You can keep the apron on, but please, join Yelena."

A cloud of foreboding had descended on the yard, as real as if a storm were moving in. Fear of these men and what they had in mind was beginning to catch in the throats of the women. One of the young boys, the one with the welt, took a foolish step forward, challenge on his face, but was immediately checked by one of the riders. "Git back there, you little whelp."

Kammers' eyes fell on the oldest woman, a graying woman of fifty. "What is your name?"

"I am Hester Prescott, first wife of Elgin Prescott, and you will burn in the ravages reserved for devils and demons."

Laughter from Kammers and his riders erupted. "We'll see who goes there first," the tall man said, immediately losing his humor.

Eleven-year-old Hazel, shivering on unsteady legs, kept her eyes glued on Yelena. Then, suddenly, she broke from the line and moved to stand by Yelena.

"That won't work," Kammers said. "You're too young."

"Hell, boss. She ain't too young fer me. She's fresh off the tree."

Kammers stared at the rider. "Rufus. Please try to appear civilized." But no further attention was paid to Hazel. Instead, the outlaw pointed to a young woman with hair the shimmering shade of sunset. "Name please."

The girl stepped forward. "Cora."

"How old are you, Cora dear?"

She did not like the *dear* attached to her name, and her eyes narrowed. "I am seventeen, and my name is Cora. Not Cora dear."

The men laughed.

"Well, Cora. I reckon we could use some of your pepper in

4

our soup. Don't we, boys?" Kammers said. "Step over there with the others."

Cora obeyed, kicking at the dirt with her boots. She normally would have been up at the stables also but had come to the house to help Rose of Sharon with the goose killing.

The tall man surveyed his selected company of girls. His eyes then turned back to Rose. "You didn't think I was going to leave you behind, did you?" He asked her name, and when she gave it, he clapped his hands. "I have just come up through the Painted Desert where wildflowers bloom after every rain. You, Rose of Sharon, are more beautiful than that whole damned country."

"You make me sick," she spat in disgust.

Kammers released a mild laugh. "We'll see. You'll change your mind once I'm all you have left."

"I'll see you dead first." She turned her back on him and started walking to the house.

"Hey! Where do you think you're going? Come back here."

"She's going to get her bag," Cora spoke up, her face set.

"Bag? What bag? What the hell you talking about?"

"Her medicine bag."

Rose entered the house, but in less than a minute, she was back, her small hand clutching a battered, leather doctor's bag.

Kammers stopped her at the gate. "This won't do. I need to know what you got in there." He motioned for Rufus Mead to dismount and go through the bag. The two remaining riders, a young cowboy called Bake, and a dark-featured, broke-down man wearing a greasy vest and shirt, name of Chauncey Simmons, watched silently.

Rufus took the leather bag from Rose, and after opening it, dug through the contents. Straightening up he said, "There ain't nothin in here but a bunch of flowers. And a couple of bottles of salve and ointments."

"Rose doctors us when we're ailing," Cora chimed in again. "But don't expect any doctoring for yourself."

"Put a gag in it, girl," Kammers hissed. He watched as Rose of

Sharon took her medicine bag from Rufus and joined the others. Like a stockman, he looked them over, grading them mentally. Then he spoke to the old woman, Hester. "Where is your husband, the honorable Bishop Elgin Prescott?"

It was Mr. Smoot, in the midst of all this jayhawking, who had wandered the yard, conducting his own search, looking behind hedges and under barrels. His narrow-set eyes finally fell upon the privy, set back a ways from the yard. In the next moment, he had the door flung open and held his pistol at the ready. He pulled Elgin Prescott from the outhouse. "Here he be, Colonel. He was plum hiding out."

Kammers laughed jovially. "Welcome to the party," he said, motioning for Mr. Smoot to drag the good bishop to stand with the others.

There was a moment of silence as Prescott was deposited amongst those standing in a line. His face was red, his jowly cheeks, free of whiskers, jiggled in fright. Hester moved to his side, reaching up to straighten the collar of his white shirt. Finally, all eyes returned to Kammers, the frightful, haunted eyes of barnyard animals before the slaughter.

"Bishop Prescott," Kammers began. "Your cowardice is shameful. Such behavior is a disgrace. Imagine what these fine folks must think of you now. However, we will address that in a moment. In the meantime, I regret to inform you that we are going to reduce your stock of horses by, let's say, a dozen. Half of them will need saddling and bitted because I am reducing your stock of wives also."

There rose a quaking of surprised moans from the group.

"I am liberating them from the hard toil you have instilled upon them."

Prescott made a feeble gesture of protest, but Hester grabbed his arm.

"Unfortunately, there is the sticky matter of marriage vows. How to break them?" He turned then and looked at the silent cowboy. "Bake, you being the newest to our esteemed company,

6

I give you the honor of giving these fine female specimens a release from those vows."

Bake sat stunned. "What? What's that mean?"

"Why, Bake, I bestow on you the title of widow maker."

Still confused, Bake stared at Kammers blankly.

"Kill him, dammit. What are you wasting my time for?"

Bake turned flush. "*But*...boss, I can't just kill someone like that. I—"

"Sure you can. It's easy. Just watch." And with sudden, unexpected speed, Kammers dragged his long Colt from its holster, and without a blink of hesitancy, the Colt roared, and Hester fell like a stone.

Bedlam followed, young people dropping to the ground in utter fear and disbelief. But Kammers quickly fired another shot into the air and called for order. Smoke from his pistol drifted across the yard, revealing horror-filled faces as they stooped, trembling.

"There now, Bake. There's nothing to it. Let's see what kind of man you are."

Bake's face was flour-white. "I...I ain't never..."

"Must I give you another demonstration?"

Prescott was on his knees beside his first wife, the dead Hester. And he was not praying, he was begging. "Pleaseee..."

"Bake?"

The cowboy pulled the pistol from his holster, slowly, carefully, aimed it at the prostrate bishop, his hand shaking mightily. He held it there a long time before finally letting his arm drop. "I can't do it."

Kammers turned in his saddle, Colt still in his hand. "Fine. I understand." Then he shoved his Colt against the chest of Bake and exploded him out of his saddle. The cowboy fell without an utterance, lying in the dust of the yard, dead face to the sky; the mortified crowd watched as the cowboy's horse danced a frantic circle around his fallen master and then ran off.

The tall man seemed enraged now. "Do I have your attention

now, you pathetic sheep?"

No one spoke. No one moved.

"Mr. Smoot, go up to the stable and get them horses down here. I want saddles for the womenfolk."

"Yessir, Colonel." And he rode away.

"Chauncey, will you do us the honor of dispensing with our good bishop?"

The dark man's face showed a sneer, and after pulling out his pistol, he shot Prescott dead, even as he begged for his life.

"You *stinking animals*!" It was Rose of Sharon. She picked up a handful of dirt and threw it at them.

Kammers looked at her. "We're all animals. Each and every one of us. You as well as me. I'm just stronger than you. You are fortunate, Rose. Your beauty saves you. But I warn you. Your tongue is a hazard to you."

He turned to the two young boys. "I am placing you in charge from this day forward. Be men now. I have given you both a valuable lesson today. Watch over these other women. I have been decent enough to leave you these."

Lampy and Mr. Smoot raised the dust of the yard again, driving down the horses. They were fine animals. It was what Bishop Prescott was renowned for—his prize horses and his prize women.

Yelena was the first to mount, pulling Hazel up behind her. Elise followed, her hands still shaking, and nudged her gray out of the way. Cora took up the reins of her favorite horse, an appaloosa she called Stella, and Rose of Sharon, putting her boot into the stirrup, swung herself into the saddle, hooking the handle of her medicine bag over the pummel. She lowered her head, trying to shake the surreal fog from her mind. This was a bad dream. It had to be.

Kammers backed his horse away from the stunned group. Hester's body was bleeding out, and it was mixing there on the ground with the blood of her husband. In the dust, twenty feet away, lay the body of the star-crossed wrangler, Bake, his vacant eyes staring empty from the other side of eternity. Chauncey, the last to return to his saddle, went to the cowboy's body and picked up the dead man's pistol from where it lay and jammed it down the front of his own waistband.

On his command, Erastus Kammers directed his small army of men and hostages up the hill and away from the yard, with the parade of horses tearing up the ground that was to be the newest garden plot. None of the women dared look back.

One mile to the east two riders walked through the grass, stretching their legs and waiting for Kammers to finish with his business. They had been posted there as a rear guard to watch against possible intruders. Toss Griffin and Frank King were more of Kammers' ne'er-do-wells gathered in his flight from New Mexico. Griffin was a two-bit mugger from dark alleys. He'd been chased out of Santa Fee when Kammers snatched him up.

Frank King, on the other hand, bore the face of a chameleon. He could charm a fox out of its den with his calculating smile, but always there was a poisonous reasoning behind that smile. Hiding behind a façade of good intentions, charming his victims with promises and flattery, he ultimately made enemies out of his friends. Frank King was a double-crosser. He didn't have to outshoot you if he could outsmart you.

Erastus Kammers and Frank King were not strangers to each other; they had once ridden side-by-side along the old outlaw trails of Nevada and New Mexico. It was King who, some years ago, had told Othello Hardy about Bishop Prescott's line of thoroughbred horses and his brood of young womenfolk. When Hardy escaped from prison, he had settled for one of Prescott's best horses. Now Kammers was raiding the entire henhouse.

"Whaddya think about this here scheme?" Griffin said. They were sitting on a fallen aspen, passing a whisky bottle back and forth as if they had no place in particular to go.

"What scheme?"

Griffin looked at King. "This here scheme. This notion of Kammers. This wonderland he keeps talkin about?"

"I know what you know," King lied.

"Come on, Frank."

They sat in silence for a mulling moment until finally King spoke. "You ever seen a water moccasin?"

Toss Griffin thought about this for a while. "I reckon I seen a few."

King smiled. "Well, there you go."

"That's all yer going to say…that he's a water moccasin? What the hell's that supposed to mean?"

"Use your imagination, kid. Whatever cautions you'd use around a water moccasin, use the same around Kammers."

Toss Griffin brooded over this. He walked to his horse and pretended to fret over his rigging. Finally, he turned back to Frank King. "If he's so dangerous, why are you riding with him?"

King broke off a long stem of grass and twirled it around his finger. *To settle a score*, he thought. But to Griffin he simply said, "Just something to do. For the time being."

Chapter 2

THE BOY WAS OUT of breath by the time he reached Marshal Boone Crowe, who was just that minute entering the Occidental Hotel for his noon meal. Doubled over, the tow-headed lad waved the handwritten note in the air like a pennant. Crowe hesitated at the door, making a stab at the paper before the wind could catch it. The boy stood panting until Crowe fished out a coin from his pocket and tossed it airborne. The boy caught it and tramped back down the boardwalk.

Crowe leaned against the hotel's sideboards and unfolded the note: *I need to see you in my chambers. Chas. Schaffer.* The aroma of potato soup and onions wafted through the doorway, and Crowe was tempted to pocket the note until after he had eaten. But then he recalled the frantic pounding of the boy's lungs in getting the note delivered, and he decided against it. Another of the judge's eruptions.

Spring and winter were still fighting it out on the Wyoming plains, but on this day, spring was winning. Wind was mild and the sun was warm, and Crowe had hoped to enjoy at least one day without the judge's harassment. Earlier that morning he had ridden out to the little spread that he hoped to call home some-day. He had been putting money against it for several years now, hoping to retire there, but things—bad things—had put a sad twist in the tail of those plans. But he still liked to ride out and look it over from time to time, trying to put a picture in his mind of what retirement might look like.

He walked to the courthouse and went directly to the judge's chambers. Judge Schaffer looked up and motioned for Crowe to sit down. "I'm hoping this is important. My steak is getting cold."

The judge ignored this, getting to the point. "Does the name Othello Hardy mean anything to you?"

Crowe sat quiet for a moment, rolling a history of names through his mind. Finally, he said, "Prison break, wasn't it?

11

About three years ago. Why? Did they catch up to him finally?"

"Unfortunately not. He pretty much disappeared. Joe Wood was on his trail. You remember Joe Wood, deputy out of Laramie? After his breakout, Othello Hardy stole a prize horse from one of those horse breeders in Utah. You know, one of those fellows that have ten wives. Anyway, Joe Wood was tracking him, but Hardy got away."

Crowe listened impatiently, waiting for the judge to get to the point.

"Something happened about that time. Because, just out of the blue, Joe Wood up and quit his marshalling job. Plum quit. He was too young for that and a damn good lawman. Something got to him, but nobody really knows what it was."

"Is this why you pulled me away from my steak and potatoes? To talk about old outlaws and lawmen who disappeared?"

"It gets worse."

"I had a feeling."

"Apparently, Othello Hardy was one of those high-strung nuts from the South. The likes of who you fought against in the war. Gentry upbringing. Parents were inter-married cousins or something weird like that. Word is he tried to set up some sort of colony of Confederate misfits somewhere down in Texas. With that came crime. Botched train robbery. Two railroad men and one passenger killed. So he and his gang, those they could capture, went to prison down in New Mexico Territory."

"But he busted out."

"Yes. Three years back."

"I've heard it done before," Crowe said, testily.

"Seems Hardy's partner in crime—another southern loon, only worse—was put in prison with him. Name of Erastus Kammers. Seems Kammers has more pigeons in his rafters than Hardy. Something of a scholar, by antebellum standards. According to the warden down in New Mexico, Kammers is like one of those exotic birds. A regular snake charmer. But deadly. And worse, he lacks a soul, if you know what I mean."

"This tale has to be leading somewhere."

"I can make it as long you want, Crowe."

"I'd rather have the short version."

"Fine. Here it is then. Erastus Kammers is on the loose again. Killed a guard in the process."

"Sounds like a New Mexico problem."

"It was. But then Kammers moved into Utah."

"So it becomes a Utah problem."

"You're not that lucky, Crowe. It is believed that they might cross the border into Wyoming soon."

"Might?"

"Well, they might be awfully close."

"Okay, dammit. Spit it out. I have a bad feeling you're going to put me in the saddle again."

"I know you like working alone. But not this time. There's a posse of Utah men heading north to meet up with you. You're to hook up with them in Wakesville, on the Utah-Wyoming border. This posse has been tracking them, but they have no authority. No legal authority. And…"

"And what?"

The judge's fingers tapped his desk. "They have no experience, Boone. They're a bunch of green church boys."

Crowe groaned. "I think today would be a good time to retire."

"This might change your mind. Turns out there are damsels in distress now too. Kammers, with members from his old gang, rode into the very same ranch that Othello Hardy stole his horse from three years ago—a ranch belonging to one of them bishops, Elgin Prescott. Kammers rode in like some avenging angel. Not only stole a dozen of Prescott's horses but helped himself to five or six of his so-called wives. All young women. Then, for good measure, he murders Prescott and Prescott's original wife. Shot down like dogs. Even killed one of his own men. For sport, it seems."

Boone Crowe sat wordlessly, pulling on his mustache.

13

"That posse needs some lawful authority. That would be you. It also needs some guidance. You again. But most of all, those young women need rescuing. Before further harm comes to them."

"Where'd you get all this news from anyway?"

"Telegrams been coming in all morning. From New Mexico. From Utah. That church down there in Utah Territory doesn't take kindly to having their peace uprooted. They don't like their bishops murdered. And they sure as hell don't like their young women kidnapped."

Crowe slapped his knees. "Is that all?"

"Not yet. There's one more thing. Turns out Wakesville is where Joe Woods has disappeared to. Has a little ranch down there with a few horses of his own. Some cows. Lives like a hermit. A thirty-five-year-old hermit. Doesn't want to be bothered."

"And you want me to bother him."

"Something like that. He may know things about this Kammers character that can help in tracking him."

"He's probably in Canada by now."

"No. He's not in our territory yet, but by all indications, he's close. He'll be here soon. You've got a window. A very small window. I suggest you get moving on this."

Crowe sighed. His appetite gone now, he was suddenly very tired.

Phony Landers was on the run, just when things were looking good for him in Wakesville. He had been minding his own business, wandering the meadows above town, nose in a book, when he looked up in time to see Bismarck Skud's bull—two tons if an ounce—barreling straight for him. It was by some divine presentiment on the part of the Lord that a stout maple tree would have been planted there, some twenty years early. He made the lower limbs just in time to feel the swish of horn and snout flash past him. It proved adequate inspiration for climbing higher.

The bull, old Skud's best, with nothing better to do, decided to camp out at the foot of that maple, snorting to high heaven. By the second day, the bull, growing impatient, began ramming the tree trunk with his thick fore-crown shaking the whole wide world. Landers hung on, but presently the maple decided it had had enough and began to lose its foundation.

Never a man for violence, but certainly nobody's fool, having lived in the wild traces of Wyoming these past two years, he produced the .38 caliber Remington from his coat pocket, and he put a devastating round of lead into the bull's stubborn head. It took two more such rounds of lead before the bull, stupid in its dying, fell first to its front knees and then over sideways like a derailed train.

Landers did not know who might have put the finger on him, but Bismarck Skud promptly printed up dodgers and had them posted all over town—PHONY LANDERS – BULL SLAYER. $50 REWARD FOR HIS CAPTURE AND RETURN. So Landers threw his books and belongings into a bag and made for the high country, where he took up residence in a shallow cave in a grove of cottonwoods above the Cayuse Breaks, as the region was called. He decided he would live there forever if need be.

His lazy, red swayback, picketed and grazing nearby, was happy with that, showing no more concern for its owner's plight than the birds in the sky. With books pillared against the cave walls, a fire of thin smoke, and a bedroll, he stretched against a friendly tree and lightened his own stress by following the hazards faced by one Oliver Twist. The perils of Oliver were beginning to wear on him, and Phony was bothered with himself for finding the villainous Artful Dodger the most interesting of all the characters. Oliver be damned to his stupid luck. He was glad he was almost finished with the monstrous book, almost too heavy to hold. He had *A Tale of Two Cities* in his saddlebag, a more agreeable burden. Out of the wind, with the sun high and warm, and the songs of the wrens and bugle birds trumpeting cheer,

Phony Landers crossed his legs, one over the other, and took rest.

Mr. Smoot played scout, riding ahead to find suitable campsites. This was no fool's errand; it was the beginning of a new civilization, or so spoke Kammers. So keeping off the main thoroughfares was critical. Still, in this wide open country staying off the beaten path was not so difficult. Soon enough they'd put Utah behind them and enter that land of promise. Kammers had it all figured.

The old outlaw came up over a rise, and with the sun at his back and to the west, he spied a world of greening prairies and red-rimmed and treed canyons, all leading to higher ground, up to the mountains. Farther up, where the snow still clung, was Kammers' fabled town, but what Mr. Smoot himself knew to be nothing more than the played-out and deserted mining town of Kitty Hart.

Smoot gazed for a long time at this spectacle, momentarily caught up in the grand and lofty dreams of his companion. If Kammers' dream came true, there would be a sharing of the women. *How else to build an empire if not with women. Lovely women. Go back as far as you like, Mr. Smoot, and you will find women. Bathsheba, Cleopatra, Helen of Troy.* Erastus Kammers' words, spoken often.

So the old outlaw turned and studied his back trail until he could see the band far behind him, their faint figures like ants amongst the grassy slopes. In that group was the long-craved flesh of women, and it thrilled him. So far the women had been quiet, eyes to the trail, worn out with fear over the murderous display shown by Kammers. That violence had made its point— Keep quiet or you could be next.

A hand to his face, Mr. Smoot scratched at his beard. He already knew which of the girls he wanted.

16

Chapter 3

ELEVEN-YEAR-OLD HAZEL WAS WEARING a simple, thin calico dress that hung to her knees when standing, but sitting on the horse as she was, her legs were exposed to the growing chill of night. She clung to Yelena like a girl drowning, burying her face in Yelena's warmer work shirt. Each of the young women were scantily dressed, save Cora, who had been up before dawn helping in the stable. Wearing pants and a worn fleece coat, she rode her horse, Stella, side-by-side with Rose of Sharon, her eyes boring into the backs of her captors, her face reddened with hatred.

More terror had been added to the women's nightmare when they saw two more riders join up with Kammers' band. A youth with red curly hair they called Toss and another man, dark in features, black riding coat much like what Kammers wore, with two pistols that blinked evil. The boy named Toss had shown noticeable agitation when he learned that the cowboy Bake had been murdered by Kammers himself. Bake and Toss had become friends on the ride out of New Mexico. Visibly shaken, Toss hung back, brooding, Frank King's words about water moccasins ringing in his ears.

Elise rode farther to the side of the group, Chauncey Simmons having herded her there, she trembling, he licking his chops. He liked her look, paler than the others, her frail fright a delight to him. He favored the helpless, the weak, the easily manipulated. In his crooked life, even the whores he had chosen were the newer girls, the younger, least experienced ones. He liked to cower over them, making them feel weaker yet. So this plain but pretty little thing with the quivering hands and nervous trembling lips was his choice. He would try and bargain with Kammers for her ownership.

The well-tanned Yelena, her russet hair with strands of blond from her hours in the sun doing her garden chores, considered her plight. She so wished Hazel had not cowed up next to her back at the ranch. She probably would have been left behind with the rest had she stayed put. But now the girl had likely put herself in grave danger. *And now I have her to protect,* she thought, *when protecting myself will be hard enough.* She felt Hazel's head bobbing against her back. It prompted her to gaze at her captors, gauging their probable brutality. The one called Mr. Smoot was gone, riding ahead. But the one riding next to Elise was a greasy bear, tobacco juice in his beard and ears full of dirt. Lampy was of the same sort. Rufus, to her surprise, was not dirty, though he was ancient. His wrinkled face showed the history of his deeds.

And then there was Kammers, the leader. Yelena saw him for what he was—a tangled web of insanity.

Peach Dupree sat in the darkness of his office, waiting, the only light coming in through a moonlit window. The aging sheriff of Wakesville fiddled with a telegram he had received two days ago from Buffalo. He'd read it fifteen times. *Marshal Crowe on the way.* Signed, *Chas. Schaffer.* Peach had spent those two days trying to pacify the three hotheaded farm boys from Utah. Three fresh youths on the trail of the widow makers.

"You can wait at the hotel till the authorities get here," he preached. "Or you can spend 'em in my jail. Cause if you ain't deputized, then yer nothin but a mob, and I'll arrest yer young asses."

"I'd like to see that," Zebadiah Wilcox said. "You and what army?"

Peach laughed. It was a laugh that had an unsettling effect on the other two young men, Marcus Wales and Giles Roman.

"Shut your mouth, Zeb," Roman said.

"Why should I? Them girls might be dead by now."

Peach Dupree spat a string of brown tobacco juice into the street. He rested the heel of his palm on his old Colt.

Roman moved close to Wilcox and spoke softly into his ear.

18

"Him?" Wilcox said incredulously, tipping his head toward the old sheriff.

"The same," Roman said with hushed voice. "My uncle was there. Saw it all. You're half stupid to have never heard that story before."

"When's this lawman supposed to get here?" This from Marcus Wales.

"Late tonight. Mebbe early morning," Peach said.

Wales looked at Roman, and Roman nodded. "We'll take the hotel," he said.

Now, waiting in the darkness of his office, Peach Dupree felt distress for his old friend, Boone Crowe. Chasing after this bunch of woman stealers would be bad enough medicine. But playing nursemaid to a trio of cocksure boys fresh out of diapers would be worse than herding cats.

He stood and walked to the window, watching the moon snail slowly across the dark sky. The old days were always at hand — the Wagon Box Fight, as it was now called, pinned down by that red devil Red Cloud, all pacified now and civilized. Peach saw the old chief face-to-face once, sitting like a lord around a table on the grass. Fort Laramie. At the snap of that old son-of-a-bitch's finger, he could have started that war all over again. Army never could figure that fox out. How a wild man could be so damn clever was as confusing to Peach as one of them Egyptian riddles.

It was much later, stretched on a lumpy bed in one of his empty cells, when Peach Dupree jerked awake at the sound of hoofbeats coming up the street. Through the window he saw Marshal Boone Crowe, shoulders sagging, climb down from a pale horse and tie it to the hitching post.

Peach opened the door in time to see Crowe beating the dust from his chaps with his sweat-banded hat. Boone Crowe stood and faced him. "You got coffee, Peach?"

"I don't presently, but I'll have it up in ten minutes. Come inside and set a bit."

"I want no part of sittin, Peach. Sittin's all I been doing for the last two days. Unless you got a parlor pillow hid somewhere."

They shook hands.

"How about a bed instead," Crowe said.

"I got two cells. Both empty. Take yer pick, Boone. I'll rouse you 'round six."

"Fine, old pard. I'll have my coffee then too."

Peach fumbled with a match to light a lamp and then turned the wick down low so that the small office expanded inside the faint glow. He heard boots slip off and hit the floor and in another minute came the musical growl of Crowe's snoring.

They had ridden into darkness, Mr. Smoot leading the way. He had found what he was looking for — a good place for resting the gang. The women were exhausted from another day of riding. Even Cora had sacrificed some of her hatred for the opportunity to get off her horse and find a place to lie down. They huddled together like a litter of bedraggled waifs, eyes heavy for want of rest, yet marked with the uncertainty of their plight. They dared not speak, communicating instead with furtive glances. Yelena settled into a rocky notch coddling Hazel in her arms, who was drunk with fatigue, her arms limp rags.

Elise shivered from both chill and fear, her eyes looking nowhere but the sandy ground before her. Rose of Sharon put her arm around her, but Elise remained stiff and unresponsive. Rose put her finger under the younger woman's chin and raised it up. Rose's affirmative nod was meant to be reassuring, but Elise simply stared, her eyes flickering blankly. All that was left for Rose to do was clutch Elise by the hand and squeeze gently. It was a gesture of false hope.

Chauncey Simmons busied himself scrapping together brush for a fire. Rose watched him with seething contempt. It was he who shot dead Bishop Prescott, the image of his dying body stenciled on her mind. She had never felt comfortable calling him her husband, nor did she consider herself his wife. She had only ever addressed him as *Sir*, her head bowed in counterfeit humility. But she had been dutiful in her chores, serving as a leader to the growing cluster of young girls that Prescott collected.

Prescott had been a breeder of fine horses and liked to fancy himself a breeder of fine women. Hester was too worn out so he paired up with Agnes and Hilda, two plain women in his brood whom he placed upon the business of childbearing. But there was something about Rose of Sharon that terrified Prescott. He seemed to shrink in her presence, even with her eyes diverted; she possessed a power over him, an influence that puzzled even her but for which she was sorely grateful. Even at the age of thirty-five, she shuddered at the idea of lying with him. But now, Agnes and Hilda could thank their unattractiveness that they were not here with the others—their homeliness having saved them.

Yelena and Cora had been deposited in Denver fresh off the orphan train from the east. Seven years separated them in age. Four years ago, when the two girls were still young, Prescott had traveled to Denver deliberately to enter into the bargaining for the homeless children. He returned with the two girls and two boys, Timmis and Rash, the same two boys Erastus Kammers had bequeathed custody of the ranch after having the bishop killed.

Prescott had been quick to marry both girls, even though Cora was only thirteen at the time, but it was Rose of Sharon again who had stood as a wily wedge between Yelena and Cora and the bishop. He was hungry for the two girls, but Rose had managed to keep him at bay, thus preserving their purity. *But now this*, Rose thought. *From the frying pan into the fire.* If she hoped to protect them against these animals, it would take staring into the possibility of her own death.

Kammers entered the circle of light, watching the flames from Chauncey's fire leaping skyward. He stared at the trembling Elise and grinned wolfishly. It was the smile of desire. The smile of demented power.

Phony Landers pressed his open palms against the warmth of his small fire. He thought about David Henry Thoreau and his deliberate solitude in the woods of New England. Phony had been a loner from the start, his luck with the fairer sex disastrous. He was not reckless enough or wild enough to hold the interest of Eastern girls for long, their own lives dull as mud. In Baltimore there was only and ever two kinds of women, the street girls, either working their charms on the unsuspecting out-of-town-ers, or the poor wenches of the factories. On the other end of the spectrum were the daughters—and occasional infidel wife—who crept the halls of their mansions, bored into stupidity by Victori-an conventions. They all wanted some form of action that Phony could not supply. His bookishness was as stimulating to these excitement-starved girls as a nap.

He still had the tarnished pistol he used to secure his escape from Bismarck Skud's bull, but it was holstered away in his little cave along with his bag of books and his bedroll. Weaponry of any kind was something of an irony for Phony, a tool that wove a contrary thread against his peace-loving nature. But times were wild in Wyoming, and after having been victimized in a stage holdup once, he decided he had best be prepared for the unex-pected. In places like Cheyenne or Laramie, or even Fort Tillman, a man could get killed just for looking cross-eyed at someone.

Landers left the fire and wandered out into the darkness to gaze at the stars. The snow was gone off the high hills and the grass underneath was already showing green away from the tree line. He stared down into the dark meadow, half a mile be-low from where he stood. To his left was a rocked-up canyon, which lead upward to an entire range of canyons. Across that same meadow, leading to the right in the opposite direction, was a copse of trees and boulders. During the day he had watched coyotes slinking through the tall grass in search of mice and other varmints. It was an admirable view, even in this midnight sky, an open meadow where he could imagine knights battling against each other. He thought of Ivanhoe, or King Arthur, caught up in a jousting frenzy. Phony was comfortable here, and he felt his little hideaway had the makings of permanence, at least through summer and fall.

He stood for a long time, listening to the night noises and then finally sauntered back to his cave where he shook out his bedding to free it from bugs or a lazy snake, and then curled in for the night.

Chapter 4

FROM HIS PORCH JOE Wood could see the rider coming through the crease of his valley pasture, heading straight for his house. He stood, the sun barely up, holding his tin cup of coffee, his breath frosty in the morning chill. Glancing toward the barn, he saw Ortega shoveling forkfuls of hay into the corral for the horses. The old Mexican had been with him for three years, rescued from a bar brawl in a little sideways border town. A brawl Ortega could not have won. Wood got to the fight just a few seconds too late to save the Mexican from getting leg-shot but in time to save his life. Two of the assailants lay dead on the barroom floor, and Wood backed the third one into a corner and pistol whipped him.

"Ortega!" Joe Wood hollered now. "We're getting company."

The Mexican stopped pitching hay and looked up the valley. "Do you know heem, Señor Joe?"

"I know him."

"Ezz he a good man or a bad man?"

"Depends. I'll let you draw your own conclusions. Come on up and get some coffee. It's fresh."

By the time Boone Crowe reached the yard, Wood and Ortega were perched on the edge of the porch, Wood with his still youthful face and handsome features, and the gray-headed Ortega with the bristly mustache.

"Thanks for not shooting me, Joe," Crowe said, unsmiling.

"It's that ugly hat of yours. And that broke down way you sit a horse that saved you." He too did not betray humor.

"That coffee looks good. You in a sharing mood?"

"I might be."

"I tried to digest some of Peach's coffee. Figured a horse ride might keep me from dying. I think he grinds nails in with his coffee grounds."

"I've had a cup or two of his poison. I know," Joe Wood said, still eyeing Crowe suspiciously.

"Mind if I step down?"

"I reckon I could allow it. As long as you don't ask me too many questions."

Boone Crowe climbed down from the saddle and walked off the morning stiffness in his joints. "You have a nice place here, Joe. You've done well. It's a true inspiration for me. I have a little place up north, a few miles outta Buffalo that has my name on it."

"Don't tell me you're retiring?"

Crowe looked off toward the corral. "Had it all figured out once. But it fell through."

"What happened?"

Crowe finally found the energy to offer a humorless smile. "I won't ask you any questions if you don't ask me any."

Joe Wood nodded. "I can honor that," he said. "Some things need to stay in the box."

Ortega had disappeared into the little house, but now he returned with a tin mug of steaming coffee. He handed it to the marshal and then stepped back and watched as Crowe took a sip. No one spoke for a full minute.

Finally Joe said, "That's an interesting horse you've got there. Pale as a dirty white sheet. How'd you come on him?"

Boone stepped to the Ghost Horse and stroked its neck. "Critter saved my life this past winter. I stole him off a dead outlaw."

"I guess that would settle the matter of ownership. You the killer of the outlaw?"

"I was."

"Still in the thick of it then, I see."

"Not always by choice.

They both drank their coffee in silence.

Finally, Joe Wood spoke. "You didn't ride all the way out here to bid me a happy day, Crowe. I'm not much for visitors these days. And I've just about run out of hospitably. State your business."

Boone Crowe wasted no time. "I'm here because I was ordered. I'm still a good soldier, Joe, so I do what I'm told."

"Who ordered you?"

"Judge Schaffer."

"Figures. I thought he'd a'been tarred and feathered by now."

"Name Erastus Kammers ring a bell?"

Wood visibly stiffened.

Boone pressed forward, telling the former deputy what he knew about Kammers' escape from prison, his kidnapping of women, and his crossing into Wyoming Territory." He watched Joe Wood's face the whole time, the paling of his features, the tightening of his jaw.

"What's this got to do with me?"

"Nothin, maybe. Only that the fella he stole the women and horses from was some Utah bishop name of Prescott."

Wood took an involuntary step backward as if avoiding a blow.

"The judge says Prescott had another visitor about three years ago. Stole a—"

"You don't have to tell me my own history, Marshal. Othello Hardy. I chased him and lost him. End of story."

"Well, this time it was worse. Kammers killed Prescott. Killed one of his wives too. Shot down dead in front of the whole brood."

The younger man closed his eyes as if some deep, forgotten pain had just revisited him.

"Now I'm saddled with a litter of Utah farm boys playing hero. They're harboring fantasies of rescuing them girls. Or women. Whichever they are. I'm a loner, Joe. You oughta know that by now. I could use your help, plain and simple." He shot a hard look at the former deputy. "And that's the end of *my* story."

Joe Wood threw the last dredges of his coffee on the ground. Then he spat.

Boone Crowe set his cup of unfinished coffee on the edge of the porch boards and climbed into his saddle. "It was good seeing you again, Joe. You've a nice place here." Then he turned the Ghost Horse back up the valley trail and left Joe Wood standing with his head bowed, his long morning shadow staring back at him.

It became obvious to Rose of Sharon that they wouldn't be riding today. The whole camp, and all of its occupants, seemed spread out and sleeping. On other mornings they would have been in the saddle already. Before it was even light, Mr. Smoot had ridden into camp with a freshly-killed antelope lying across a pack horse. For an hour she could hear the old hunter and his counterpart, Lampy Dixson, skinning and preparing the meat. There was a rustling of pots and pans in the dim twilight, and after a while, the fire was fed and the smell of roasting meat wafted through the canyon camp.

Rose had spoken bitterly to Kammers the night before, telling him that the girls were cold and they needed coverings. Kammers had responded by ordering the man named Rufus Mead to fetch the saddle blankets and give them to the ladies. His calling them ladies had a sick sort of hint to it that angered Rose all the more. The blankets smelled of sweaty horseflesh, but their warmth was welcome.

Yelena was the first to catch Rose's eye as the day brightened. There was a steely determination in her expression, one that both encouraged and frightened Rose. Yelena was a strong young woman, loyal to little Hazel. But Rose feared that that loyalty might become a costly element if someone tried to take advantage of Hazel.

Yelena laid the young girl's sleeping head onto the blankets and slowly scooted herself close to Rose of Sharon. Both women lay back, pretending to sleep. Finally, Yelena whispered into Rose's ear. *My gardening knife is in my boot.* This news caused Rose to blink. Her first thought was to dismiss the usefulness of a mere gardening knife. But then she reminded herself that a knife might be the deciding factor in the end. Whatever the end might be. She turned to Yelena's ear. *Keep it there. Now is not the time.*

Both women turned suddenly to see Chauncey Simmons

standing over Elise. She was still sleeping, a Godsend for the fearful girl, and as she slept, Chauncey kept staring. Finally, he put the toe of his boot against the bottom of her shoe and tapped. Elise jerked away, immediately looking into the brute's eyes, and she screamed.

"Wake up, little doll," he said, ignoring her shrieks. "Say goo' morning to yer new husband."

Instantly, the camp came to life. Mr. Smoot stepped away from his fire and stood before Chauncey. Even though Mr. Smoot was far older that the big man, he showed no fear. "That'll be enough of that, Simmons. Git yer ass back to the hole you crawled out of and shut yer mouth."

All the girls were awake now, watching. Chauncey stood like a dumb beast. "She's mine. This un here is mine."

"She'll be yours when Colonel Kammers tells ya she's yours. And I doubt he ever will. You're too damn ugly and stupid to be paired with someone as beautiful as this little darlin'. Or any of them."

Strangely, Chauncey did not protest these insults. Had it been Lampy or Rufus who'd addressed him, they would likely be dead or crippled by now. But the ancient Mr. Smoot seemed like a giant himself, as if clothed in some sort of mysterious armor. Chauncey blinked stupidly, took one last hungry stare at Elise, then lumbered off into the far reaches of the rocky canyon, the echo of his empty threats circling the rock walls.

The screams finally brought Kammers into the circle of firelight. "My apologies, ladies. Chauncey is a pig for manners. And you, little Elise, you certainly have a pair of lungs about you. They could hear you screaming on the streets of Richmond, I am sure." He stepped to her and with an outstretched hand, touched the terrified girl's cheek. "You are a pretty one. I would hate to have to cut your tongue out. But that scream of yours is indeed a weapon. If I hear you scream like that again, I'll have to take unpleasant measures."

He turned and spoke to Lampy. "How long before breakfast?"

"Thirty minutes, Colonel. Not a minute more or less."

"Fine Lampy. That is excellent news." Kammers retreated then into a crevice in the rocks and sat down. He pulled a small book from his saddlebag and opened it. Even in the dim light the women could see his lips moving, mouthing the words of Shakespeare.

Marshal Boone Crowe was in a dour mood that not even a breakfast of steak and potatoes could brighten. As he ate, he addressed the three young men from Utah, each standing before him like school children.

"We leave in an hour. I'd prefer you went back home and helped yer pa plow the upper forty. But Sheriff Dupree said you were a stubborn, if not stupid lot. You're determined to die young. And I reckon that's yer natural born privilege."

The three young men hated him already.

"So listen up. I am the boss of this here circus. You will do what I say when I say it. I am used to being obeyed. I've seen a hundred of your like die on the first day of battle. History didn't start the day yer young asses was born. You are not invincible."

He took another bite of steak and chewed it while the others watched. Zebadiah Wilcox fairly snarled.

"How many rifles we got,?" Crowe asked.

Giles Roman stepped forward. "I have one," he said. "It's a Henry."

"Henry's good for close up. Not so good for long distance. But," he paused, "that's what I carry. That's how I generally fight—close up."

The very thought of close quarters fighting caused Roman to shudder.

Crowe looked next to Marcus Wales. "I've got a shotgun," Marcus said. "Two barrels."

"Shells?"

"Nearly a boxful."

"Another thinking man, I see."

Crowe, in spite of his frustration, was nonetheless enjoying this interview. He was grilling raw recruits again, just as he had twenty years ago, before the predawn slaughter called Cold Harbor.

"What about you?" he asked Wilcox.

Zeb Wilcox simply stepped forward and touched the tips of two mismatched Colts, one on each hip.

"Those yer daddy's?"

"What if they are?"

Crowe ignored his flippancy. "You ever fired them before?"

"Shore I have. Plenty of times."

Wilcox's two young partners looked at him.

Crowe sighed. "Shootin rabbits and coyotes ain't the same as shooting mankind. Especially if that mankind is shooting back."

Wilcox bristled. "You tend to your shooting, Marshal, and I'll tend to mine."

A pain of prophesy seemed to stab Boone Crowe in the gut. He looked down at his remaining breakfast and tried to swallow down the sensation.

Just then Peach Dupree burst through the door of the hotel dining room. He saw Crowe and hastened to his table. "You got a visitor, Boone."

The lot of them walked out onto the street where Joe Wood sat his horse. Wood's face showed a mood similar to Crowe's. His horse was equipped with a bedroll and swollen saddlebags. A Sharps rifle butt shown from its scabbard. His words were terse. "Here's how it is, Crowe. Swear me in. You can take this pack of tenderfeet with you and follow Kammers' trail. But I go alone. I've a couple of hunches. But I won't be slowed down by you or these pups."

With his speech over, Crowe sent Peach to fetch a badge and a Bible. "We better do this before he changes his mind."

The swearing in was quick, done while Wood remained

mounted. He turned his horse to go and then turned back. "There's an old deserted mining town in the mountains. Played out years back. I heard it mentioned once by one of Hardy's old henchmen. Fellow named Smoot. They could be heading that way."

With these words out, Wood flanked his horse, and Boone Crowe watched him ride away.

Chapter 5

"Gather round, my little darlings," Kammers ordered. Everyone had eaten chucks of meat from the charred antelope that Mr. Smoot had killed in the night. The sun was full up now, and the day was warming, with the canyon walls blocking the spring wind.

"Com'on gals. It's time you officially met your new caretakers."

One by one the women reluctantly stood and formed a tight group. Elise needed help rising on shaky legs. They clung to each other like a litter of kittens about to be drowned. Each of the men formed a semicircle around them, each seeming to gape in lustful hunger.

"As you may have heard me proclaim, you ladies are the chosen specimens that will accompany us to our kingdom on the hill." Kammers let this absurdity sink in.

Hazel pressed closer to Yelena, eyes wide in confusion.

"Mr. Smoot, please step forward and say hello to the ladies."

As instructed, the wiry wrangler stepped from the back of the circle, a gray-whiskered grin on his face. His eyes panned the women but stopped on Yelena. Mr. Smoot bowed politely to her and then stepped back.

"Mr. Smoot here is my civilized lieutenant. You need have no fear of him. He is polite as a tulip. He will serve as your nanny. Anything you need, Mr. Smoot here is at your disposal."

"Lampy Dixson and Rufus Mead are a pair of old war veterans who served side-by-side with my father, the honorable Carlisle Urban Kammers, Lieutenant Colonel, 25th South Carolina Regiment, deceased."

Kammers, who had been too young for the war, took a breath after this long dialogue, while Lampy and Rufus stepped forward and took their turn in the limelight. Like Mr. Smoot, they were older, but unlike him, both were clothed in greasy trousers and shirts. Lampy wore a studded vest and Rufus, in his awkwardness, flashed an empty, toothless mouth, his chin nearly touching his nose.

Chauncey stepped forward without an invitation and lumbered up to Elise, who nearly collapsed under his foul stare.

"Mind your manners, Chauncey," Kammers said. "You're scaring the girls. If you continue to show your brutishness, I'll have to put you in chains." The other men laughed at this, and Chauncey turned on them, eyes red with hatred. The big man sulked off into the shadows.

"Toss Griffin is new to this party. He has yet to prove his worthiness."

The young man stepped forward hesitantly. He did not like Kammers' remark, but then neither did he like Kammers himself. His old riding partner, Bake, was killed by this crazy bastard, and now all he wanted to do was escape from this fool's errand. But he didn't want to escape alone. He wanted one of the women to go with him. Feeling a need to prove himself, he strode directly up to Cora, who stood with tightened jaw and flaming eyes.

Cora stood her ground, staring back at the boy with his wide-brimmed straw hat and plaid shirt. He still had a cowboy's bandana dangling from around his neck and a Colt pistol shoved into a deep holster.

"Howdy…ma'am," he half-stuttered to Cora.

Without warning, Cora's hand flashed out, knocking Toss Griffin's sombrero off his head, sending it sailing to the ground.

There was a chorus of laughter behind him. So, turning, Toss reached out and grabbed hold of Cora's long hair. But before he could do anything with it, Cora's fist shot out and collided hard against Griffin's ear. Thrown back, the young wrangler, still holding the girl's hair, pulled her toward him. This time Cora bowed her head and stove herself full-strength into his chest. They both fell to the ground, Cora on top. She hit him again, her little fist finding Toss' eye socket. All around the laughter rose. A dust flew up, circling the two combatants as they rolled in the dirt.

The other women stood in horror. Was Cora trying to get them all killed?

Finally, Kammers motioned to Mr. Smoot and the old man grabbed Cora by the back of her shirt collar and hoisted her to her feet, her claws bared and slashing. Mr. Smoot gave her a shake and dragged her out of fighting range.

Toss was still on the ground, showing bloody furrows on his face from Cora's fingernails. He stood up, stunned and humiliated. The laughter continued. He searched the battle site for his hat, but before he could get to it, Cora, still fuming, reached it first. With one swift motion, she planted it on her head, and with a bedeviled stare, dared the boy to take it away. Toss did no such thing. He merely turned away, trying to laugh it off himself. In his parting attempt at dignity, he said, "Hell boys, that's my kinda girl." This too was met with roars of merriment.

Frank King watched this circus with concealed amusement. Kammers, he knew now, had surrounded himself with a court of clowns, Mr. Smoot being the one exception. When they finally reached wherever it was they were going, he wondered just how many of them would be left standing. King was sure of one thing, though—he would be there to face Kammers in the end.

Joe Wood knew where he was going because he knew where Kammers was going. Boone Crowe would have welcomed this information, but knowing the marshal, he figured the crusty old lawman would want to end this thing quickly. To Wood's way of thinking, he had to get to Kammers before Boone Crowe put a bullet in him. He only needed a day or two, provided luck was on his side. If he could get to Kammers first, then he might be able to finally catch up to Othello Hardy. And Hardy was the real prize, the man Joe Wood wanted to kill, more than anything else. Killing Hardy may not erase Wood's own misdeeds, but it would give him a small degree of peace—a peace he hadn't known of three years.

It was a canyon where Hardy had once made a sub-camp at a time when Kammers was riding with him. They had operated out of this cleft, rustling and robbing, the perfect place to hold up until things cooled off. The few foolish ranchers who had tried to follow them into this hideout never came out. It was from this rocky notch that Hardy made his final run. The outlaw had been alone by then, on one of Prescott's most beloved blacks, a beautiful beast bred to run. And run it did, carrying Hardy all the way to Fort Tillman. Only hours behind the outlaw, the country around Fort Tillman was where Wood had made his mistake—the mistake that continued to haunt him.

The reinstated deputy had left Wakesville and rode through the day and into the night. If Kammers was in front of him, then there was a strong chance he'd slipped his gang and the women into this cozy hiding place. The leaves were just now coming onto the trees, making visibility into the purple canyon more difficult to see. But if Wood could pick his spot, he might still be able to look down into the narrow slot of red rock pillars and catch sight of his prey. But now he had to stop again. He had pushed his horse to the limit. By early morning, after a rest, he would be there. If he could put a scare into Kammers, he might be able to flush the outlaw out of his hole and into the open. From there it would be a hit-and-run battle until he could get close to Kammers. And that's all he wanted.

Marshal Boone Crowe pushed the farm boys hard, hoping they would get discouraged and call it quits. Like Joe Wood, they rode all through the day and into the night. There were many tracks in the loamy earth, but because it was cattle country, it was difficult to tell if they were on the trail of Kammers and his captives, or just another herd of beeves being shuffled from one high pasture to another. The posse had already cut across several trails that led nowhere.

Finally, Crowe decided that Kammers might be using these trails himself to cover up his own tracks, using them for a while and then cutting off to confuse anyone following. Surely Kammers must know that someone was following.

The young man, Giles Roman, rode abreast with Crowe, watching him. After hours of this, Boone Crowe calculated that the boy was copying him, studying the marshal's habits and style. Crowe counted this as a good thing. Of the three, Roman was the only one who appeared to possess any sand. And sand would be needed if they ever caught up to Kammers and his gang.

Once, when they had slowed their horses to a walk to rest them, Crowe asked Roman why he was there risking his life.

Giles Roman seemed embarrassed at first, and then some awkward words finally stumbled out. "One of them girls, marshal. I've known her a good spell."

"Were you part of that Prescott bunch?"

Roman shook his head. "Neighbors," he said. "But I saw her in church. And sometimes at socials."

"Are the two of you…betrothed," Crowe asked bluntly.

Roman flushed. "Oh, no sir. I mean…well…I guess I was fixin to…"

The boy couldn't finish.

Crowe thought about his own bad luck with women. With *the* woman. Eva. The only one he had ever loved. Now this shy young man was looking at the same lousy circumstance that Boone Crowe had looked at some years back—a search for a woman who was in grave danger. He wanted to comfort the boy, but he had no words of comfort in him.

"What about the others?" the marshal asked after a while.

Roman looked over his shoulder at the other two farm boys. They were a good distance back. He shrugged. "Marcus' pa made him go. Said we owed it to Prescott to bring the girls back. Even though Bishop Prescott is already…well, already dead."

Crowe listened.

"Marcus argued with his pa, hoping to change his mind."

"Kind of young to be chasing after killers, ain't he? He seems not more than a kid."

Roman stared straight ahead. "It's what they do."

Boone turned and looked at the boy. "Whaddya mean, it's what *they* do? Ain't you part of *they*?"

Giles Roman looked over his shoulder again. "I ain't decided yet. I got my own ideas, but…I keep 'em to myself."

Crowe was starting to like this young man. "So, what about that other one? The big shot."

Roman coughed a laugh. "You mean Zebadiah." The boy thought for a moment. "I can't say for sure, Marshal. I've known him for a long time. But he's always been this way. Kind of thinks he's better than the rest of us. I don't want to say nothin bad about him. Even though, he has a way of rubbin folks the wrong way."

"Is he as tough as he pretends to be?" Crowe wanted to know what kind of people he had riding with him, and he figured he'd ask tough questions straight up. "Or is he just a blowhard kid trying to prove himself? If that's the case, he could be dangerous."

Giles nodded at the lawman's conclusions. "He could be," he said. "Maybe."

Joe Wood found his spot. He'd been here before. Darkness had edged its way into the treed ridges and into the sloping hills to his right. But the old familiar signs were still there—the big boulder that stood like a sentinel a half-mile from the pinched break in the rocks below, wide enough for a horse to slip through. That was only the entrance; there were other ways out, including simply following the canyon's natural upgrade through the trees until it leveled out on a plateau, miles farther on.

Wood dismounted silently. He was pretty sure Kammers would have at least one picket out, watching the back trail. Most likely that would be Mr. Smoot. *That old bastard never sleeps,*

Wood thought. He busied himself finding a place for his horse, a place out of sight, and then, taking his Sharps out of its sheath, he walked downhill, skirting the same hardpan path he had followed three years before until he was close to the hidden canyon's opening.

A fire is what he hoped to see, some orange glow, maybe with some sparks flickering into the dark sky. If he could decide exactly where they were camped—if they were even here—it would tell him where he could shoot from in the morning. He wanted to put the fear in them. And a well-placed bullet would do the trick.

He found a boulder-strewn incline to his left and quietly picked his way higher. If Mr. Smoot were anywhere around, Wood would be a sitting duck. It was a risk he'd have to take. He moved this way, stealthily for five minutes, and then, rounding a sharp rib in the rocks, he saw what he was looking for, the soft pumpkin-colored silhouette of fire against rock.

The deputy stared into that faint radiance for a while, calculating. Finally satisfied, he picked his way back to the fork and then to the boulder where his horse was.

"We found 'em," he said, speaking softly into the ear of the red mare. The animal nodded knowingly. From his saddlebag he retrieved a Navy telescope, the single treasure left to him from his grandfather's sailing days. He held the instrument in his hands as if it were piece of breakable porcelain. "Tomorrow," he whispered.

Chapter 6

SMOKE FROM CHAUNCEY'S ROLLED cigarette circled the oily man's face. He watched the women hungrily through this cloud, his pig eyes glaring like a mongrel dog's. The sun crept up the canyon rim, finally spilling over and throwing crimson shadows against the rocks. Lampy stirred the fire while Rufus filled the coffee pot with water from his canteen. He threw a handful of grinds into the pot and set it on the flames. Behind him he could hear Kammers stirring, his customary morning ritual of coughing and spitting.

Rufus felt at home in these surroundings, this roughing it. It reminded him of the war, which had been his salvation from a life spent underground in the mines of Pennsylvania. Sure, he'd fought for the Union, but he held no bitterness toward those he had fought against, the Rebels of Virginia. He hated the mines, and yet, here he was, following Kammers up yonder into another mine. The old Kitty Hart mine, silvered out plenty of years back. He'd help the Colonel get his little empire off the ground if he could, but he had no plans of going into the deep, dark earth ever again.

Colonel Kammers, who was never a colonel of anything, only inheriting his dead father's rank out of the odd Southern habit of birthright transfer, had himself an idea that a better world existed somewhere. Rufus had seen the man reading strange books, and talking about fellows like Alexander the Great and Cornwallis somebody. But it didn't matter to him what Kammers read, so long as he kept the old Yankee fed and out of the rain.

Rufus watched as Chauncey looked over his shoulder to see if Kammers was watching. Then he slunk over to where the women were huddled in their saddle blankets. The brute said nothing, only stared down at the sleeping Elise, her skin so pale and invit-ing. He turned once more and glanced back at Kammers; then looking back at the girl, his head suddenly exploded into a burst of red. The sound of the shot came a second later, followed by the echo of the Sharps bouncing off the rocks.

For an instant, Chauncey stood in stupid death, the whole camp around him flying into immediate chaos. When the big man finally fell, blood from his split head was flung onto Elise's legs, and the girl screamed like a woman scalped.

Strangely, Rufus did not move. Crouched in front of his coffee pot, he watched as everyone scattered. He'd seen things like this before. But the women, as if not traumatized enough, pressed themselves deeper into the rocks, Elise kicking at the fallen Chauncey with the heels of her shoes, trying to get away. To Rufus' right he saw Frank King and Kammers, pistols drawn, trying to calculate where this shot had come from and waiting for the sound of the next one. But there was no next one.

The whole band lay flattened on the ground, save Rufus. He was too interested in the scene around him; in the dead Chauncey, who was no friend of his anyway; in the girls, the likes of which never interested him either, knowing the lot of them would rather die than lay with a toothless buzzard like him. The boy, Griffin, still hatless, stared with open eyes at the corpse. Lampy, too, though an old soldier himself, seemed unusually perturbed.

No one moved or spoke for a long time, with the girls peeking their eyes from around their blankets like forest creatures, and Kammers with an expression of anticipation. Frank King stood back in the shadows, a place Rufus had decided the man liked best.

Finally, working his gums like a steam engine, Rufus hollered out. "Coffee's ready."

Phony Landers heard the shot, the quaking of it as it reverberated up from the belly of the canyon to his left. It sounded like a hammer-blow more than a shot, but the husky, unexpected echo of it told him someone besides himself was out and about. This was not welcome news.

In his years of tramping the country, he had found that keeping his own company was something to value. His history with the fairer sex had been dismal, though in his quiet moments he still dreamt of some sweet companionship. But the woman he dreamed about was faceless. No doubt she didn't even exist. He envied the luck of Mr. Darcy in *Pride and Prejudice* for finally conquering the love of Elizabeth Bennet. Some days he saw himself as an English lord, while other times an Arab sheik. But in the end he was simply Phony, a tag given him in his earliest years because of his constant daydreaming. His friends accused him of never being himself, only some character from one of his books.

If someone were invading his place here on this hill, it might mean packing up once again and pulling out. He watched the shadow of the sun creep across the meadow below, and his mind turned back to the distant echo of the gunshot. He finally concluded that it must have been a hunter shooting at game. There were birds above and around him now, warblers or meadowlarks, and he let their song woo him to sleep. Letting his head rest against an aspen trunk, he closed his eyes.

Something changed in the air, a stirring, a sixth sense, and Phony jerked awake. Some time had passed, for the shadow on the meadow had advanced. He shook off his drowsiness and stood. There, to the far right of his little grassy amphitheater, was movement. Horses. And men.

Phony counted. Four riders and a pack horse. He watched as they dismounted in a grove of trees bordered by a string of boulders. From his vantage point, they were the size of mice. Then, to the far left, a simultaneous glint of movement where the meadow broke into the sharp pillars and clefts of the rocky canyon, a flash nearly invisible but for a wink of metal against the sun.

First the shot, Landers reasoned. Now riders on his right and a blink of movement on his left. Something was astir.

43

Mr. Smoot clambered down from his roost in the rocks where he had tried to catch sight of Chauncey's killer. The whole camp had been turned into an uproar of nerves—a lone shot that split the ugly brute's head like a pumpkin. Then silence. But Mr. Smoot hastened back into the camp because of what he'd seen to the south—horsemen. He went straight to Kammers and reported. "We're gettin company, Colonel. Riders."

"Posse?"

"Can't figure no other reason to be here."

Chauncey Simmons' body had been dragged away, but his blood remained, and Kammers looked at the smear of it on the rocks now. "That explains this," he said, nodding toward where the big man fell.

"We figured they'd be on us. Just not this quick." Mr. Smoot stood obediently, waiting for instructions.

Kammers looked at the women, huddled like ducklings. "How many did you see?"

"Five maybe. Six at the most."

"What were they doing?"

"They were bunching up in the trees, best as I could tell. Might be making an early camp. Or jist resting up for a night ride. I don't reckon they know we're here."

"What about this?" he said, pointing to the bloody rocks.

"Advance scout, likely, Colonel."

Kammers considered this. "If that's the case, then we're in the stew pot."

Lampy Dixson came forward and joined the conversation. "How 'bout old Rufus and me give 'em the old cavalry charge. Nothin makes a man turn coward like a chargin horse and an old fashioned Rebel yell. It plum puts the jitters in a fellow."

Kammers shook his head. "They call that suicide, Lampy. Forget it."

Lampy laughed. "Well, I'm plum itchin to do something, Colonel. This sittin around is like ta turn me old. I rode into many a charge like this with the Black Knight, old Turn Ashby. We had 'em runnin, ha, sure 'nough."

Frank King, listening from a distance, wondered if such a thing could work. And even if it didn't, all the better. Two less to have to deal with later. He watched Kammers fretting over what to do next, his teeth grinding on his bottom lip. Suddenly, Kammers spun around and shot a look at King.

"There's daggers in men's smiles," Kammers said, quoting *Macbeth*.

Frank King smiled and then bent forward in a formal bow.

Mr. Smoot watched as the two men acted out their scene. He knew something of Shakespeare, but he knew more about hatred, and it was thick now as brush smoke.

Phony Landers was not the only one who had seen the glint of Mr. Smoot's weaponry flashing against the sun. Marshal Boone Crowe had seen it too. He pulled up the posse with a wave of his hand. "Move the horses into that dark notch in the trees. They need to be out of sight."

Giles Roman was the only one to comply. After dismounting, the marshal watched Zebadiah Wilcox and Marcus Wales jostling with each other over some jerked meat that Wilcox had pulled from his saddlebag. It became a schoolyard contest, and they elbowed and shoved each other playfully.

Crowe bristled. He led the Ghost Horse into the trees beside Roman and his horse. Then he took the lasso from his saddle and walked back to the others. Using the coiled rope like a whip, he stuck the two boys across their shoulders. He whipped them till they scattered.

"*What*...hey...what's the big id—" howled Wilcox. "Git them horses into the trees like I told you. Do it now!"

Wilcox touched a welt on his face. "You can't do that."

Boone struck him again with the rope, and the boy fell back against his horse, which by now was turning skittish. Moving in, Crowe grabbed Wilcox by the collar and threw him to the ground. "This ain't a church picnic," Crowe hissed. "These men are killers. And they're probably out there." He pointed across the meadow to where it turned into a rocky line of rim rock. "When they shoot, it won't be fried chicken and biscuits, you worthless whelp. It'll be lead. Now move it."

Zebadiah Wilcox seethed with hatred. Wales, by this time, had taken up the reins of his horse and led it into the trees where Roman was watching the action. Wilcox stood and tried to grab the reins of his unruly horse. It shied and Crowe watched the boy struggle. Finally, the horse moved close to Crowe, and the marshal retrieved the reins. He spoke brief, tender words into the horse's ear, and then, without further discussion, handed them to the flustered Wilcox.

The boulders were waist high, forming a natural fortress. Crowe saw signs of others having camped here, but they were old. It had not been Kammers. He was pretty sure of that.

Roman came to the marshal's side. "What are ya figuring, Marshal?"

Crowe was silent for a while, and then he said, "Someone's up there in those rocks."

Giles Roman followed Crowe's stare where it carried across the long meadow to the ridgeline. "You think so?"

"I gotta consider everything. Kammers can't travel too fast. Not with a half dozen women and no spare horses. I think we're finally on the right trail."

Roman took off his hat and scratched his head. "We cut off the trail, didn't we?"

"You boys did. But last night while you was dreaming about sugarplums, I kept on the trail for another couple of hours. It led up there." Crowe pointed to his left, to a high hill, grassed and shadowy under a thick, tree-lined crown. "On the other side of that hill is the opening to that cluster of rocks. They're either camped in among those canyons, or they kept moving across the flat. But like I said, they can't move fast forever."

They stood side-by-side, their eyes panning the terrain before them. The meadow from the ridgeline to where they stood was flat and grassy. But even as they watched, they saw two horsemen emerge from a dark cleft in the rocks. They were a good distance away, but it confirmed what Crowe had suspected.

"Whaddya think, Marshal?"

Crowe didn't answer, just stared at the two figures. In time a third horseman appeared. "Get your Henry, Roman."

In a matter of minutes, the old lawman had his untried posse of young pups situated in defensive positions amongst the boulders.

"You don't think they're gonna try and rush us do you, Marshal?" This from Marcus Wales. His face had turned pale, and he held his shotgun with jittering hands.

"It's been done before. Best to be ready."

"Why would they want a fight?" Wales went on. "It don't make sense."

"Has anything they've done so far made sense? Trust me, son. The men on those horses don't think like you and me. They think as madmen think."

"Why don't we just go after them then? There's more of us." Wilcox had finally joined the discussion.

"Numbers don't always matter."

"They ain't moving. They're still jist sittin there," Wales said, his voice aquiver.

"Let 'em come," Wilcox said with bravado.

Crowe hated the situation he was in. He'd been on the wrong side of cavalry charges in the war. And he'd been on the right side of them. Saddled with this group of greenhorns, he knew those three riders out there could easily ride right over the top of them. He had no idea what would happen if lead started flying. He looked at the three riders and prayed they'd just go away.

But they didn't.

"Oh, hell," Crowe said. "Roman, it's you and me with the Henrys. Wales, that shotgun's no good unless they're right on us.

Twenty feet. One barrel at time. Then reload. Fast. Wilcox, don't waste bullets. And keep low. Your pistols might be pretty, but they're only for close range. But if they get close, pour lead."

Lampy, Rufus, and Toss Griffin moved out into the meadow, slow at first, gauging the distance. They could see movement in the boulder-strewn shadow of the trees. Lampy laughed and Toss cursed him for it. He wanted no part of this, but he feared Kammers' temper if he disobeyed.

Halfway to the trees, the three riders stopped. Lampy and Rufus held council from horseback. "I got a bottle of red whisky says they turn tail and run at the first shot," Lampy boasted.

Rufus put his toothless mouth to working, his gums making a slapping sound. "Like you Johnny-boys did when we run ya outta Gettysburg."

"You tryin to work me up, ain't ya? Ha. Wal if Lee'd a listened to Longstreet, we'd a won that spree. You ready?"

Rufus' mouth became a wide, black hole of mirth. "I was bornt ready, Lampy, you old sombitch. Ha." He looked over his shoulder. "You ready, Toss my boy."

Toss Griffin made no sound. He allowed his hand to touch the scratch marks left on his face by that witch-girl Cora. His heart was pounding for her.

"Fine then, fellers," Lampy said. "Git yer irons out and put the spurs to 'em."

The charge began. At full gallop they raced across the meadow.

Crowe watched them come. He hated the whole idea of this. Cover meant little in a running charge like this. If these boys panicked, he'd be all alone. He glanced at the sky, thinking for a second that it might be Cold Harbor all over again. The sky on that second day of fighting was the same sickly blue, only there was cannon smoke so thick on the ground that seeing the sky was a thing of pure chance and beauty.

The riders came on abreast, two of them riding without reins, rifles lifted to their shoulders. Their first bullet tore through the posse's midst like a hornet, striking the tree behind them. Crowe raised his own Henry, and after putting a bead on the center rider, he squeezed off a shot. It struck the ground, throwing up a tuft of grass.

"Shoot, Roman. Find a target and shoot." Crowe's voice seemed spooky in his own ears, and then suddenly he heard a blunted yip to his right followed by the sound of a body falling. He didn't turn to look, only fired again. He heard Roman's Henry roar now too. They fired together again, and again, and finally they saw one of the riders pull up his mount. But the other two continued on. They were getting closer.

Then came the blast from Wales' shotgun, too soon, the pellets flying off harmlessly. But the thunder of it stopped another rider. Still, the one man kept coming, pushing his horse now, his crazy howl rising above the noise of hoofbeats and gunfire. It was a yell Crowe knew all too well, and still heard in his dreams. A damn Rebel yell. *How long before that war is finally over?* he wondered. He levered another shell into the chamber of his Henry, took careful aim at the moving target and fired. Like a circus acrobat, the rider somersaulted off the back of his horse and landed on the ground. He was less than fifty yards away.

The first rider to give up was hightailing it out of range, but the second man sat on his horse as if in shock. Slowly, he started walking his horse toward his fallen comrade, but Roman's rifle barked again, causing the horse to bolt sideways. The man pulled hard on the reins and turned the animal in a full circle. He did this twice before turning it back toward the other fleeing man and rode away, not hurrying.

The sudden quietness was startling. When Crowe finally

turned, he saw Wales sitting on the ground, the shotgun across his lap, a thin wisp of smoke coming from the barrels. Then he saw Wilcox, his arms stretched out at his sides, his legs splayed like a wishbone, a dark and bloody cavern where his eye socket had once been. Both pistols were still in their holsters.

Wales was on his knees now, vomiting onto the ground, retching over and over. Roman looked at Wilcox's body, and he pivoted on weak knees, hollow-eyed and pale. Crowe looked away without a word and stared at the man lying in the meadow barely fifty yards away. *Another five seconds he would have been on us*, he thought.

"Roman, get Wales together. Talk to him. He needs a voice now. Then put something on that boy's face so we don't have to look at him. I'm going out to see what we've got."

Giles Roman steadied himself, laid his rifle across the top of the boulder he had been shooting from, and moved to Wales, who was crying now. Roman shucked off his coat and placed it over Wilcox's head. He turned and watched Crowe move across the grassy field to the fallen outlaw. The marshal had his Colt drawn, and he walked with a sickening slump to his shoulders.

There was a rasping sound, and Crowe knew it for a lungshot. Lampy lay face down like a ragdoll, limp and coiled.

"You nearly had us," Crowe said. "If yer partners hadn't abandoned you."

Lampy coughed and blood spattered the grass. "Did I get any...a you?"

Crowe didn't answer. Lampy's rifle was in the grass twenty feet away, but Crowe knew there was a pistol, and he wanted to be careful here. He'd seen many a dying man have one last shot in them. He moved forward carefully and put his boot on Lampy's forearm. "Where's yer Colt?" he said.

Lampy coughed a bloody laugh. "Hide and seek, *Mar*...shal."

Boone Crowe hooked a boot under Lampy's ribs and flipped him over. The pistol was there, but it was still holstered, and the dying man was too weak to use it, so Crowe reached down and yanked it out.

"Have the women been harmed?"

Lampy shook his head.

"Where's Kammers headed?"

The outlaw said nothing.

"You don't owe him anything. He done got you killed for yer trouble."

"You...*you* the one kilt...Chauncey?"

"Not me. You're the only one I killed. Who's Chauncey?"

But Lampy was fading fast. Blood was seeping out the side of his mouth now, and his eyes were showing a glassy film. "Can ya..." The man gasped, sucking at the air. "Can ya...hold ma hand, Marshal..."

Marshal Boone Crowe holstered his Colt, knelt beside the fallen outlaw, and took the man's hand in his own. "If you got any peace to make for yer deeds, this'd be the time."

"Too...*late*..." The outlaw's grip slackened and fell away.

Standing, the marshal looked down at the old Reb, shot to hell and likely heading there this very minute. *Sometimes there's no saving them.* These were the words of the one-armed preacher, who would have had better words for this dead man than Crowe had. But even that might not have been enough. He wished his friend the padre were with him now. He did not want to go back to the others. He did not want to look at the dead Wilcox again.

Chapter 7

PHONY LANDERS SAT IN mortified silence, staring down into the meadow where the most bizarre drama had just been acted out before him; as if he were a spectator at a play. Balcony seating. A panorama of violent tragedy. He heard the soft pulse of the gunshots, the men riding, then the one falling. He had even seen into the shadowy cluster of boulders where the men were firing back from, and the one who was thrown backward onto the ground. He'd seen it all.

One of the men walked to the dead man, knelt, and then picked up the slain man's weapons and horse and walked back to the others. Landers recalled his reading of *The Charge of the Light Brigade*,and he realized the futility of that charge had just been acted out before him. The two riders who fled had escaped into the rim rocks, drawing down the curtain on this bloody performance.

A cold wind came through the trees, and Landers saw, in the distance, a blackening of the sky. His horse, grazing freely under a long picket rope, raised its head. It stomped on the ground as the wind stirred its mane. *Spring storm*, Phony thought. Never trust the Wyoming weather. He moved back to his little grotto and sorted through his belongings, fetching a coat. He shook it out and put it on. He'd have to move his fire closer to the shelter. Night was coming early.

Erastus Kammers was stuck in a dream. His father was on horseback directing the slave workers into the cotton field, the one by Nettle Pond. His sisters and their friends were all around him on the veranda dressed in their finery, giggling. It was Swan's birthday, and she was the prettiest of all his sister's friends. Even the sunshine seemed to follow Swan. But, as dreams do, the whole scene shifted into darkness, and through flashes of lightning, he saw the army of Sherman foraging the fields, the very house around him razed. He came out of this dream with a jerk and a shout.

Rose of Sharon saw Kammers buffet against his blanket, kicking himself awake. She studied him, his mad, blinking eyes. He seemed like an animal now. Not a human animal, rather an actual fanged beast, with a look on his face that reflected both torment and hatred. He emitted a low, guttural growl.

Earlier, when Rufus and Toss had ridden back with the news that Lampy, and his foolish notion of a cavalry charge, had not only nearly led them into an ambush, but that he got himself killed in the bargain, Kammers became unhinged. He knocked Toss to the ground and made an attempt to do the same with Rufus, but the old Yankee prune showed his agility and dodged away.

Cora had watched Toss Griffin scramble off like a whipped pup. *Twice beaten*, she thought—once by her and now once by this creature Kammers. Hazel too huddled with saucer eyes. On the farm she had never seen violence like this. But in the last several days, she had seen a lifetime of it. She looked up at Yelena and mouthed a confused prayer for their protection, something she had been taught by Rose of Sharon, a simple thing that started and ended with, *in our need*. She said it now again, like a mantra. Yelena, hearing her whisperings, brushed back the girl's yellow hair.

Kammers stood finally and began his pacing. He called Mr. Smoot to his side, and together they spoke in low tones. Mr. Smoot pointed up the canyon, moving his hand like a slithering snake, indicating the terrain that lay ahead.

"The Kitty Hart is about forty, fifty miles straight up that way," the old scout said. "On the flat, that's a day and a half. Up this here canyon, it's near a week. It'll be slow goin, Colonel, but now we know we're bein chased, it offers some options."

"What options? I *need* options."

"Cover mostly. If we follow the canyons, they'll be followin behind us. They'll be fightin us uphill. It'll be hit and run. Not another one a' those fool charges."

Kammers gazed up the canyon. It was still dark, but the moon gave him enough of a picture for him to consider. Behind them, Frank King pretended to sleep. It didn't matter to him which way they went. He was here for the long haul. Hell, he might even stick around long enough to earn Kammers' trust. A little mining town filled with young women had its benefits. As well as a band of has-beens to send out pillaging the countryside. He was finding himself getting into the spirit of the thing. That woman they called Rose seemed just his type. He'd have to make sure no harm came to her—spoils go to the victor.

The dead Zebadiah Wilcox was wrapped in his bedroll and lay across his horse. There had been no campfire, so the others had worked slowly and wordlessly.

Finally, Marshal Crowe spoke. "Wales, I want you to take this boy back to his kin."

"Me?"

"You have no business being here anyway. I know yer pa sent you. Now I'm sending you back."

Wales flashed Roman a disapproving glance. What else had Giles told the marshal? That he was scared. Hell yes, he was scared.

"But..."

"Don't argue with me, son. You had yerself a good long look at Wilcox there. He was burnin to prove himself a hero. Now there he is." He nodded to the body.

Roman was grateful for the darkness. His own stomach was a twisted knot, but he felt safer sticking with the marshal. Wales was being ordered home, by a United States Territorial Marshal.

Even Wales' father couldn't argue with that. He might finally see his son as having some worth.

"You can't think of that boy anymore. He's gone," Crowe said. He knew he was being callus, but it was necessary to the moment. "I'd like you outta here before daylight. I don't trust this pack of coyotes. They may double back. So rustle now. Put some miles behind you." Crowe hated speeches like this. Any kid with half a brain would be dancing a jig to get the hell away from this mess.

Wales threw the saddle on his horse, cinched it up, shoved his shotgun into its scabbard and mounted. Roman handed him the reins of Wilcox's body-burdened horse and turned to go. "I could help, Marshal," Wales said.

"I know you could, son. You already did. That scattergun blast is what turned those other two riders off the mark. Otherwise we'd a'had our hands full."

"You mean it, Marshal?"

Crowe spoke like a father, though he had never been one. But he saw the boy's need. "Yes, Marcus," using the boy's first name. "Roman and I are standing here because of yer part. That's a fact. Now git yer ass moving."

Wales slowly turned away then, and inside a minute he was lost to the darkness.

Someone was out there. Phony Landers could hear hoofbeats coming up the back slope of the hill. A rider was picking through the trees. There was no longer a moon; it had finally surrendered to the push of the building cloud front. Landers took his pistol and moved away from his fire and into the trees. After what he had witnessed down on the meadow, he knew trouble was afoot.

He paused under the black shadow of an aspen and listened. The sound of hoofbeats had stopped. Minutes passed and Phony felt a clammy sweat break out on his forehead. He watched for movement in the trees but saw nothing. Then suddenly, the click of a revolver's hammer and the soft, cold press of its barrel touching the back of his neck.

"Let's walk out to your fire now. Real careful like."

Phony obeyed, taking one careful step after the other. The pistol he was holding hung limp at his side. Reaching the campfire, he stopped.

"The pistol. Drop it."

Phony let it fall to the ground.

"Turn around. Slow like."

In the darkness, Joe Wood's badge drew a glare from the fire. Phony stared at it before he looked up into the face of the deputy. "Whaddya want with me?" Landers asked.

"What are you doing up here? Are you a lookout?"

Phony Lander's throat tightened. "A lookout? For who?" His eyes remained fastened on Wood's pointed pistol.

"You tell me."

Landers, with his hands high in the air, tried to nudge away his fright. "I can't tell you anything…because I don't know what you're talking about."

"Kammers," Wood said.

"Excuse me?"

Neither spoke. Wood, still covering his quarry, moved toward the cave and took a quick glance inside. It was mostly dark, but from the ruddiness of the firelight, he could see a book lying open on a blanket and a scattering of crackers and an unwrapped haunch of meat. He had interrupted supper. There was an organized pile of litter too.

"How long you been here?"

Landers sighed irritably. "A couple of weeks," he said. He realized now that he'd been tracked down for the shooting of Oliver Skud's bull. He furrowed his face in defeat.

Wood was calculating, though. A couple of weeks ago Erastus Kammers was still in a New Mexican prison. Or had just broke out. *So who the hell is this guy?* he wondered. He stepped back to

57

Landers. "Put yer hands down."

Phony obeyed hesitantly.

"What's yer name, tinhorn?"

"I guess I'm caught then. I'm the one who killed Skud's breeder. I'm Landers."

"Oliver Skud? You? You're the...*ha*. You're the famous bull killer?"

"Isn't that why you're arresting me?"

Joe Wood holstered his pistol. "I ain't arresting you. Hell, I don't give a damn about old Skud's bull. You coulda killed that sonofabitch himself for all I care. He's nothing but a thief. Country would be better off if he was coyote meat."

Landers stood in confused relief.

"And you've been hiding up here?"

Landers nodded.

"Pick up yer gun before it rusts."

They stood in the awkward darkness, the fire fading. "Who... who's this Kammers?"

The humor left Wood's face. "I'm after him." He gave Phony a brief account of what he knew, the few facts he'd heard from Marshal Crowe but keeping sure not to say too much.

"He stole women?"

"I saw 'em. They were holed up in that canyon over yonder. I killed one, I think."

"You killed one of the women?"

"I might have. If I did, I didn't mean to. I was hoping to kill a big ugly brute standing over 'em. I spied him through my telescope. Then took a bearing and shot."

Landers looked at the deputy. "I heard you. Heard your shot." The echo of it seemed to ring again in Landers' ears. He told Wood what he had witnessed in the meadow below. "It was theatrical. And...deadly."

"Crowe," the deputy whispered. "So, he's that close." This news reached him with mixed blessings. He still hoped to reach Kammers first. A dead Kammers would be of no use to him.

But now, with the marshal dead set on flushing him out, Wood needed to consider his options. He knew this canyon for what it was, a longtime hideout. But he wasn't certain about what lay beyond. When Othello Hardy got flushed out, the outlaw had headed straight east, not west. And Wood had followed him that way to the railhead at Fort Tillman. But this canyon wove northward, veering west. *If Crowe manages to chase Kammers up into that canyon*, he thought, *then I've got to be on the other end, waiting.*

"You familiar with this country?"

Landers didn't answer.

"Up north? Up beyond these gorges?"

The relief Phony had felt after learning he wasn't under arrest began to evaporate. He was feeling uncomfortable again.

"Speak, man," Wood demanded.

"Well, there's a couple of towns. Very small. Pretty scattered. A few small farms in the clearings. More ravines. There's a hot springs up there somewhere."

"People?"

"Not many."

"What about this canyon?" He motioned into the darkness. "Does it open up onto higher ground?"

Phony Landers pretended to calculate, even though he already knew the answer. "Well," he said slowly, "I reckon it does. It's a good ways, though."

"Take me there."

Here were the damnable words Landers had dreaded. All he wanted was to stay right here, anchored to this spot. To wait out the fine spring, summer, and early autumn in this secluded alcove of trees and birds and solitude. He doubted he would ever be bothered with another shootout in the meadow below. Besides, he had *Gulliver's Travels* to read yet.

"Do I get a vote in the matter?"

"Leave yer gear here. You can fetch it later. I want to travel light and fast."

"How 'bout I draw you a map?" Phony bargained, but Deputy Joe Wood was already moving into the darkness to collect his horse.

Chapter 8

BOONE CROWE WOKE FROM an hour's troubled rest. It was not yet dawn, and he felt worse than before he closed his eyes. This was already a sleepless chase, and it was going to get no better. Crowe had let Roman curl under his blankets while he had kept a keen ear for any sign of retaliation by Kammers' party. But the night had been still. He hoped Wales was well on his way back to Wakesville. He didn't envy the boy's mission, of returning the dead Wilcox to his kin, and then having to face his own father for having been ordered off the hunt.

Dawn birds frolicked in the treetops, and Crowe tried to clear his mind of all things troubling. He thought about his deputy, Rud Lacrosse, back in Buffalo. The young man was in the dreamy throes of romance. Paige Canady had put her brand on Rud, and he was lassoed in a big way. And who could blame him. Paige Canady was the prettiest thing this side of a shining mountain sunset. But these thoughts always led to Eva, so he abandoned them.

He thought about Wales again, the timid Utah farm boy. He'd overheard the young man talking to Roman one night, fretting over the iron sanctions of a constantly disapproving father. *Some men are born to hardness*, Roman had told him, sounding the part of sympathetic sage. And when Wilcox had been killed—a random shot from a desperate man riding horseback—Wales had fallen apart. And who could fault him for that. Crowe remembered his own baptism by fire, trying to make himself part of the Tennessee soil, lying flat as he could as Johnny Reb slugs flew over him like a nest of hornets turned loose. The men on both sides of him were killed without comment while he lay there eating dirt.

Somewhere into those rim rocks were five women. Girls more like it, he reasoned. Those married were now widows at the hands of Erastus Kammers, a man he'd only heard about from Judge Schaffer. But he felt he'd run into his likes before. Douglas Starkweather came to mind. The old Southern renegade had burned out like a Roman candle. A man never knows how or when his end was at hand. If he had a chance to get close enough to Kammers, there would be no time for banter or barter. He had been a marshal too long to toy with chances.

At first light he and Giles Roman would try and find the entrance to that canyon and follow Kammers to hell if need be. He rubbed his palm across his face, his whiskers like quills. *But then there's the women*, he thought. That'll make it a whole lot tougher.

Mr. Smoot took the lead, followed closely by Kammers. Rufus and Toss were next, with the women trailing in single file up the narrow track of rocks and stony edges. Farther back was Frank King, with instructions from Kammers to keep a close eye on any girl trying to escape. He didn't want to tie them to their saddles, but he would if he had to.

Yelena rode in the front of the women, Hazel behind her with arms wrapped tightly around her. Cora, atop Stella, was after her, jaw set as if she somehow had control of her own destiny. Elise rode in front of Rose of Sharon, holding onto the pummel of her saddle as if it were an anchor. She was beginning to see herself as a survivor now. The ugly animal that taunted her was dead, and though it was a shocking and bloody death, she counted it as a blessing. In a dark place in her heart, a place she previously did not know she possessed, she found herself reveling in the sight of his bloody head being split open. But it was still Kammers himself whom she feared.

Rose thought about her Georgia upbringing and the Cherokee grandmother who had raised her. The old woman was the perfect paradox of womanhood, delicate in touch, with a beautiful face of softly wrinkled skin. She had taught Rose all she knew about the medicines of the plant world, how and when to use them, and the healing powers of each. But there was a wildcat in that old woman's spirit. When Rose was just growing into her own beauty, there was a neighboring litter of boys, ruled by a sluggard father, who tried to take Rose into their clutches. The old woman took a finely honed hunting knife to the first boy who grabbed at the girl, lopping off his hand at the wrist. The old man came next and received a hammer blow to the head for his trouble.

Distant, fuzzy memories of this endearing woman, beleaguered by years and hardships, filled Rose's head, and she prayed that she herself might somehow have been granted the gritty spirit of her grandmother. It was a kindly neighbor a few years later who found Rose huddled in a corner of their hovel, her arms around her dead grandmother. Months of shuffling from home to home followed before, at the age of thirteen, she found herself aboard the orphan trail, heading into the mysterious, wide open west. She was raised under the watchful eye of Hester Prescott, herself young at that time. But something welcome, though unexplainable, had made her a confusing hazard toward the advances of the bishop. He kept his distance as if she were some sort of bedeviled bane.

The trail, narrow and craggy, wound slowly upward, and the fog, which laid upon the land like filmy cotton, put a chill on the women that could not be shaken off. The horse's iron shoes clacking against stone was the only sound, and it seemed to have a numbing effect on the women—hammer blows that drove deep the peril and plight the women were facing.

Rose knew, as clearly as if it was painted on this fog, that the malicious desires of these evil men would eventually prevail, and all things desperate would be staring each of them in the face. She must find a way to prepare the girls. It would require a courage she hoped she possessed—knowing in the end it would mean a faceoff with Kammers, to the death, if need be.

The first rain came in a raging force, throwing a sheet of water into Marcus Wales' face, lifting off his hat and spinning it from his head. He dismounted, and while trying to manage the reins of both horses, he fought his way through the torrents back to his hat and snatched it from the ground. He peered through the pelting rain, looking for shelter and pulling the horses, he made for a thicket of low-branched firs.

In spite of these efforts, he was soaked to the skin by the time he was able to reach a canopy of thick, high branches. With freezing hands he hastened to pull the saddle and bridle from his horse and stake the animal to a tree trunk. He stood for a minute, dripping wet, and stared at the other horse, the one bearing Wilcox. He shuddered, more from distress at being alone with this once alive but now dead man than from the cold rain.

Hobbled with indecision, he set about scraping up any dry kindling he could find. There were old and decayed branches and cones scattered on the ground where so far the rain had not penetrated. He made a pile, and within a few minutes, a welcome blaze licked at the edges of the murky afternoon. But there was still the matter of Wilcox and what to do with him. Night was only an hour or two away, so Wales decided to unburden Wilcox's horse out of sheer mercy for the beast. But his mercy for the dead braggart was waning, so he simply grabbed the rope that bound him to the saddle and pulled, letting Wilcox's body fall to the ground. He tied the horse next to his own and wiped them down with their saddle blankets. Then he began removing his clothes. If he left them on the chill might take him over and he too could be dead before he reached Utah.

Wearing only his boots, Wales built up the fire, stringing his clothes on the branches closest to the fire's warmth. He shook out his bedroll, and in spite of its dampness, he crawled inside. He watched the lump that was Wilcox's corpse as a new and foreign emotion creeped into his mind. He had no name for it because he had never felt it before. But as his body heat began to rise, so too did this new thing. It felt like a furnace in his breast, and all his

64

shivering stopped.

The rain outside the perimeter of his shelter continued to fall with a fury, drowning out all other noise save this other strange fury, this new one burning him up inside. His father's face materialized in the shadows, his scornful expression darkening even the darkest part of the night. *I knew you couldn't handle it*, the condemning words came. They snapped like the fire's crackling flames. *This was your chance to be a man and you failed. You come back whipped. At least Zebadiah, dead as he is, died fighting like a man.*

Marcus thought about the kidnapped girls. He knew them all from church and from the summer socials held down by the river on Sunday afternoons. There was timid Elise and hardworking Yelena. Marcus had heard his father complain about how Bishop Prescott always had his pick of the pretty ones. *One man shouldn't have it all*, Nyth Wales had said. *I'd give half my stock away for the one they call Rose of Sharon.* This seemed like a running theme with his father, and now with this new red emotion coursing through him, Marcus wondered if there might have been more to his being sent out with the posse. It wasn't just about making him a man—it was about the girls. About the women. They were widows now. All of them. And that changed everything.

Marcus Wales stared at the body of Wilcox, soaking up the rain, the ground around his form bubbling into puddles of mud, and he swore out his hatred for him. For the first time in his life, he realized he could hate someone else besides just himself. For all of Wilcox's bravado, his end had come like a whimper, an insignificant flicker from this world to the next. And now, as if light had suddenly covered the darkness of this place, Wales understood fully the only path left for him to take.

In a frenzy, he threw off his blanket, and still naked, he tramped through the downpour to the body and let loose a high, sharp howl of redemption. He fell to his knees, the rain funneling off his back, and he began digging in the mud with his hands. The earth was soft, and he scooped up handfuls of muck, digging like a creature possessed. He dug and scraped, finding the cavity deepening, his breathing that of a savage mandrill. *I owe you nothing*, his distempering mind raged. Deeper and deeper he clawed, his fingers and hands caked with black soil, lifting, pulling.

A distant coyote's scornful lament brought him back. He looked at the hole and judged it deep enough for a blowhard like Wilcox. Seizing the bedding the dead man was wrapped in, Wales yanked the bundle into the pit and began shoveling back the pile of dirt. It was a shallow grave, and he wondered if perhaps the coyote would soon be feasting on Zebadiah's flesh. It mattered not. Not anymore. Let his kin wonder. He was free of it now. And he was free of his own father. Free, because as he dug, he knew he was never going home again.

Standing over the grave Wales mouthed the parting words— *from mud you were made, to mud you return*. Then, covered in the slick, brown mud of his diggings, he marched to the saddlebags that held Wilcox's double holsters with the miss-matched Colts and strapped them around his naked waist. Wiping his hands on his bedding, he lifted both pistols from their sheaths, and pulling back the hammers, he fired into the darkness, the soul-cleansing muzzle flashes lighting up the shadows where his father's words now fled into shrinking whispers.

It was the Wyoming that Joe Wood knew all too well, a land of surprises. Even as darkness came rushing toward them, they could see the snow coming with it, white against the dark land. He and Landers had shouldered their way to the west of the canyon's drop and found their way onward, into a plain of rolling, grassy hills. But now the devil weather was coming to meet them, like a fighter unafraid. Both men tied down their hats with their bandanas and pulled their coat collars up tight against their necks, but when the snow finally hit them, it piled onto their shoulders like heavenly fleece. They were riding into the very heart of the storm with no cover in sight.

Phony Landers thought about what brought him to this far-away place on the map. He was a long way from the Chesapeake country where he walked like a pilgrim through the woods and back places. He knew his head was in the clouds, and he made no apologies for it. Rather than work in a shipping office in Baltimore for another solitary day, he signed on with a surveyor's crew that was hammering its way through the northern plains ahead of a Minnesota railway line.

Half starving one winter, and only twenty-two years old, he took up teaching in a school near St. Paul. Every evening as he chopped wood for the school's iron grate stove, he watched the sun go down in pink and yellow polish. His wanderlust next took him one territory at a time, a town at a time, drifting until starvation again drove him back into a schoolhouse somewhere. And that is how he came to know the very country they were set upon now, facing a springtime fury of snow.

Phony looked over at Joe Wood, the deputy's head bowed so the brunt of the storm could not attack his face straight on. He did not like the lawman. Not much anyway. Right now he only wanted to be back in his cave, out of this weather, his fire lapping at the frigid air, a cup of hot coffee and *Gulliver's Travels* across his lap. Instead, he was in a manhunt he wanted no part of. *Or is it a woman hunt?* he thought. Was this a Scott fable, *Ivanhoe* maybe? Reading the story as a young boy, it was Robin of Locksley who stove its way into his imagination, prompting him to take fencing at school, and later archery. He never used it, though, as his fantasies always faltered in parallel with his courage.

The entire world was white now, and even riding side-by-side, the deputy was nearly invisible in the gauzy realms.

Chapter 9

IT WAS EASIER NOW, with just the two of them, Giles Roman following Boone Crowe like a shadow. But the sudden change in weather was putting a hampering delay on their progress. Through a day-long downpour of sleet the two men finally found the big boulder that marked the opening to the canyon. The icy wind slashed at them as they picked their way slowly into the belly of the rim rocks, and Crowe saw the futility of trying to track in this weather. The canyon snaked upward into high country. If Kammers was following it to its top, Crowe and Roman would have to keep a keen eye out for ambush. But this weather made that impossible.

In the gray storm, they found the outlaw's deserted campsite. Crowe dismounted and moved his Ghost Horse beneath an overhanging ledge and motioned for Roman to do the same. The camp was a mess of discarded victuals, animal bones, tin cans, and grease paper. A long smear of black blood was being washed from the rocks, and Crowe followed it into a narrow notch where the body of the killed Chauncey lay, wedged like an oyster in its shell. Bending close, the marshal saw the parted skull and the empty eye sockets where the ravens had feasted.

The bed of stones that had been the old, dead campfire showed a pile of wet ashes and a litter of unburned twigs. Giles Roman kicked at this, wondering where in this mess the girls had been gathered. Gloom, bigger than the storm, burdened him, and he searched the muddy grounds hoping to find some sign that would lift his heart, but there was nothing. Kammers had not kidnapped them to kill them. His plans seemed worse than death.

Roman tried to picture each of their faces in the leaden sleet. Yelena, her buoyant lilt when she walked. Steely-eyed Cora, whose beauty was undeniable, but her pigheadedness a threat to any man. Elise, shy and stunning, rarely smiling, her brown hair shiny as a colt's. Hazel, the child. *What business did they have with her?* Roman feared this thought. And Rose of Sharon. The medicine woman. He had known her from boyhood. From the day she plastered his chest with mustard paste to open up a cough that had plagued him for weeks.

The iron sky darkened so Crowe pulled the saddles from the horses. Dry wood was scarce, but Roman scrounged enough to get a coffee fire going. Crowe heated salt pork in a small pan, and the two men leaned against the only dry wall of rock they could find and settled in for the night.

"Whaddya figure, Marshal?"

Boone Crowe rubbed at his whiskers. "It'll be cat and mouse from here. And I'm not much for that kinda fightin."

"They're up there, though, ain't they?"

"Signs seem to show that. Unless they came out the way we came in. But I doubt it. They're movin up these canyons, same as us. Only they've got a day, maybe two on us."

"How many you reckon there are?"

"Hard to say. That big one up in the crevice there. His head looks like the handy work of Wood's Sharps, but can't say for certain. Anyway. He's dead, and the one we killed night before last. So they're minus two."

They sat in silence for a while, trying to get comfortable and listening to the pounding of the sleet against the rocks overhead. Finally, Roman asked, "Was you in the war, Marshal?"

Boone Crowe didn't like talking about the war, only thinking about it and not much. It had a way of forcing itself on him at unexpected times. But he liked this boy. He was eager to learn and working his way into trustworthiness. As they moved their way closer to Kammers, the success of killing or capturing this bunch might end up resting on this young man's shoulders.

"I was."

Roman stammered for his next words. "That thing...back there. It was the first time I ever...well, used my rifle for anything like that. I never shot at a person before. And...never saw a dead person before either. Much less someone I…well, someone I *knew*."

"It won't get easier."

"No, I don't reckon it will."

The sleet was gradually turning into snow, and Crowe marveled at the unpredictability of Wyoming springs. He loved this country but longed to find a more peaceful way of enjoying it. He was not dirt poor. Every once in a while there came to him reward money for the capture or killing of wanted men. And a small pension from his service as an officer in the army. After the war, he'd served in the chase after Shelby and his Confederated raiders who fled to Mexico. All that money he'd left untouched, until a few years back when he made a down payment on a little spread outside Buffalo. It was to be his retirement ranch, with a wife and the whole shebang. But…

His thoughts ventured no further on the subject. Instead, he said, "The war made lifetime killers out of a'lotta men. Something about everyday war that eats at the brain."

"I was scared, Marshal. Is that something to be ashamed of?"

"Bein scared saved many a lives. If a man ain't scared when he's on the receiving end of hot lead, then he's likely to end up like your friend Wilcox."

"He weren't much of a friend. Not really. But it was still a shock. Seein him kilt like that."

"Multiply that by a hundred and that's war," Boone offered thoughtfully.

"When was you the most scared?"

Crowe allowed a humorless laugh. "From the beginning to the end. Scared the whole way through."

"Wales is more my friend than Wilcox is…*was*. But Marcus, he ain't got it so easy. His pa is a devil to put up with. Marcus never gets it right, it seems. And he was pretty scared too. Is that why you sent him back home?"

"Bein scared doesn't mean yer a coward. I never figured Wales was a coward. But we're going up against hardened men.

I didn't care much for the idea of having two families burying their boys."

It was Roman's turn to laugh. "What's that say about me?"

Crowe smiled in spite of himself. "I had a hunch I couldn't have driven you off with a switch. You must have some kinda investment in this hunt."

Giles Roman blushed. "Well...*I*...I do know all the girls."

"I figured as much. Women can be great motivators." Even these words were painfully spoken. The images of Eva were as ghostly and as frequent as those of the war.

Roman watched the snow falling with a purity that the rest of this escapade seemed to lack. "What's the closest you been to bein killed?"

Crowe was waiting for this question. It was always second in line to the most-asked question—*how many men have you killed*? A question that had no answer. "I've been shot at and shot through. With bullets and arrows. I don't have a particular preference."

Roman was silent, thinking.

"Closest was a crossroads called Cold Harbor, I reckon. Only 'cause it seemed to have no end. It was a pigeon shoot. And we were the damned pigeons. I never got hurt bad there. But the possibilities were greater. Old Grant seemed to think we were made of steel. Afterward he knew better. The field was piled with dead. It shocked even him."

A sound like a moan betrayed Roman, and he gave a shutter that was not from the cold.

"I had my horse killed out from under me," Crowe went on. "It was hand-to-hand in some parts of the line. There's a strange kind of heat that goes with that kinda fighting. Shooting across a field is altogether different than staring into another man's eyes. It's plum wild. The whole war comes down to you and him. You don't know what's goin on a foot either side of you. You catch a glimpse of eternity in his eyes even before you kill him. Strange. It has a feel of brotherhood to it. A brotherhood of savagery. A killing kinship you might say. Where both yer lives have reached

72

their purpose. It's…it is…"

Boone Crowe wavered in sudden embarrassment. He'd gotten carried away. The sound of his own voice had startled him, and he was both afraid and ashamed to go any further.

Giles Roman sat wide-eyed. The picture had been painted.

The storm was riding hard on the backs of Joe Wood and Phony Landers. They were lost. Barely could they make things out beyond the muzzles of their horses. Snow piled atop their shoulders and covered the necks of their mounts, heads bowed low as if ready to drop. The deputy seemed in a daze, his own head bobbing as if in a slumber. At one point he leaned too far to his right and nearly toppled from his saddle, but for Phony's sudden grip on his coat sleeve. The schoolteacher was close to blindness himself, but he did his best to squint through the storm's violence.

Phony's bare fingers were stiff as carrots, and his nose ached with the pain of needles. He silently cursed Joe Wood for dragging him into this boondoggle, and the remembrance of his cozy cave agitated his nerves like a festering boil. He guessed that the deputy's present fatigue was from his sleepless ride to get wherever it was he was going. It had now taken its toll. But Landers knew he was not much better off. The cold was pulling every ounce of strength from him too.

It seemed they had been riding in this white nightmare for days, not hours, and yet any form of shelter, if there was such, had evaded them in the blinding surrounds. Again Wood nearly toppled, and again Phony saved him from the fall. They were riding slow and close together, otherwise the deputy would be lost underfoot, trampled into the drifts by his own horse. He suspected the lawman was close to freezing. A strong desire to sleep was working its way into his subconscious, and he wondered if maybe they shouldn't just dismount and rest in the snow. Only for a little while.

Landers shook it off when he saw the twinkle in the distance, faint enough to have the feel of a dream. He blinked into the netherworld. It blinked back. His father's old adage came to him now — *Son, never follow a light into the dark or you'll never return.* As a boy he'd had visions of tramping to the end of the world, or worse, into the devil's lair. *Satan is a tempter to young children.* But regardless of his father's axioms, he continued to plod through the storm toward the flickering light.

Looking over at Wood, he decided to take up the reins of the deputy's horse as well because of the fear that at the last minute they might get separated. The light was getting closer. It was the yapping of a dog that finally told him they had come upon a house, and the light was coming from a square of window, the blowing branches of a leafless tree playing with the glow. Too cold to holler, he rode directly up to the door, deciding the crunch of a dog's teeth might actually help thaw him out. But before he could fully dismount a long, narrow wedge of light appeared where the door of the house was opened. It yawned only a couple of inches, just wide enough for the barrel of a shotgun to peek out.

"Stay put, mister." It was a woman's voice, but the gun stopped him mid-stirrup.

"We're plum froze, ma'am." He could not see her for the glare.

"Who are you?"

"My name is Phony Landers. And this other fella. He's Deputy Marshal Joe Wood. We're outta Wakesville." His words came in a shiver, freezing in the air.

"Are you his prisoner?"

"No, ma'am. I'm just an unlucky schoolteacher. I'm serving as a guide for this lawman. But he's like to die any minute now." And indeed it appeared that way, as Wood was now bent nearly double over the neck of his horse.

"My son is here with me. And he has a pistol too." She called the growling hound into the house, opening the door wider for it to slip through. "Lift your man over to the dog run." She tipped her head to her left. "There's a chair there to put him in. Till I can get a better look at you."

Phony eased the near limp frame of Joe Wood down from his horse and half dragged him to the mentioned chair. The dog run separated the main house from a smaller room built off as a storage space or added bedroom. The woman materialized behind them, suddenly appearing through the streaking whiteness as if a ghost. Even now Landers wasn't sure he was living it or dreaming it. Wood's head came up then, startled as if from his own nightmare, his eyes wide and wild. He started to stand, but Phony intervened. "Stay put. We're about to reach heaven."

Over his shoulder he saw the so-mentioned boy taking the two weary horses off yonder into the blizzard, presumably into a shelter. "The horses," he said.

The shotgun was black against the snow. "Pull off that hat. I want to see your face."

Phony obeyed.

"I want those gun belts dropped onto the boards. I'll pick 'em up myself. Do it slow-like."

Again, Phony obeyed.

"And your partner too."

Landers turned to Joe Wood and whispered into his ear. "We've been invited to the tertulia. But we must disarm first. Now don't go killing me. But I need to unfasten your pistola."

Wood nodded stupidly. He moved to unfasten his holster, but his numb fingers failed to make the action work, so he surrendered the task to Landers. While he did this, the woman had opened the door to the disjoined shed and motioned them inside. "There's a pallet for him," she said. "You'll have to stretch on those grain bags."

"Paradise, ma'am. And much obliged we are to you. Now, them horses…"

"Kip is putting them in the barn. He'll give them a handful of oats, which you'll pay me for. And he'll rub them down, which you'll pay him for."

"Today, ma'am, I'd promise you a ticket to the Paris Fair if there was such a thing."

"I'll save you the trouble, Mr. Landers, by refusing you ahead of time." Her words were spoken without humor.

Frank King had the face of a weasel. It was not altogether unhandsome, it simply possessed a mask of distrust. It began with a leering smile that would set a cactus on edge. He turned his horse and was riding through the falling snow back to where the women were. Their clothing was soaked, and they were visibly shaking. As he drew up alongside Rose of Sharon, he pulled a bedroll from behind his saddle and offered her the blanket. She glared at him.

"Give it to Yelena. She's got the girl." She spoke as if addressing a snake.

"How about I give it to you, and you can give it to her?"

Rose gave no answer, so he tossed the blanket across the pummel of her saddle. She immediately slowed her horse until she was next to Yelena, and then she opened the blanket like a cape and wrapped it around Hazel. It was big enough to cover Yelena's shoulders too. The two women exchanged a nod. Frank King lingered a moment longer and then rode away.

"What was that all about?" Yelena whispered.

"Working favors, I'd say." Her voice was husky from the cold, but she kept it low. "How's the little one?"

"She's shivering. The blanket will help." Yelena pulled the musty blanket closer. "Thanks, Rose."

"We can't go like this much longer. We'll all be dead from pneumonia."

Just then Kammers could be seen riding toward them, emerging through the snow as if entering a stage in his fantasy from behind a white curtain. He flashed a jaunty smile as he approached, his horses working sideways in a spirited prance.

"Evening ladies," he said. He grabbed for Rose's free hand with a swiftness she could not avoid. He gripped it in his own and then lifted it to his lips. "All the perfumes of Arabia will not sweeten this little hand."

Rose pulled her hand away. "You're disgusting."

Kammers laughed, his narrow features widening with his mirth. "I have no spur to prick the sides of my intent, but only vaulting ambition, which o'erleaps itself, and falls on the other."

Yelena spit on the ground, and Rose of Sharon laughed.

Kammers face clouded. "I'll not be mocked. I've saved you from a life of bondage."

"Is it not bondage to have us freezing to death in this cold," Rose fired back. "All you'll get are the corpses of five frozen women."

"Ahh, but your surprise awaits you, maidens. Why, just five minutes ago Mr. Smoot delivered some splendid news. There is a hot springs not a half hour further. You will all be able to lounge in its fountains, warm your souls, and cheer your spirits."

Rose and Yelena exchanged glances.

"I leave it to you to tell that wild cat. And the silent one." He said this, nodding in the direction of Cora and Elise. "And," he went on, "there is an old Indian lodge where you can sleep under shelter. There is a fire pit for warmth, and Rufus has brought us a superb specimen—a slain stag."

Both women saw the madness in Kammers, in his voice, in his bearings, and in his deranged flamboyance. It chilled them, even more than the cold snowy wind.

Chapter 10

MARCUS WALES BROKE CAMP before daylight. The rain, which had turned to snow in the middle of the night, had finally ceased, and now, even in the gray light, the young man saw great wet clumps of it falling from the tree branches. He left the crude gravesite of Zebadiah Wilcox without regret. He had the dead man's pistols strapped to his waist and his horse, saddleless now, following behind on a lead rope. He felt free. Free of Wilcox and free from the scorn of his father. Let the old man wonder for a lifetime what happened to his son. It didn't matter anymore.

For the first time in his memory, he heard a cheerfulness in the music of the meadowlarks. The skeleton aspens were silver with frosty buds, and they seemed bunched like statues in a park. He marveled at them. Coyote tracks in the snow zig-zagged ahead of him, following the tracks of a lone hare. The sight of it brought him back to the chase, to the girls, and to the marshal. They would be long gone from where Wilcox had been killed, moving after Kammers into the somewhere of Wyoming. *But where?* he wondered.

A pang struck him. The face of Cora Prescott came to him in the middle of the night, her jaw set in jeering ridicule. She was the only one who did not keep her distance when they picnicked at the river. The only girl who challenged all the boys to out-race her, or beat her at games. Zebadiah caught her by the pigtail once, and after lifting her, he tossed her in the river. She came out like a wet cat, arms flailing to no account, all her punches missing. But by sunset that day, as everyone was packing up baskets and folding blankets, it surprised no one that Zebadiah and Cora were found under a tree, making cow eyes at each other. It was old Hester who scolded her into sensibility, reminding Cora that she was the wife of the bishop, Elgin Prescott, and that encouraging the Wilcox boy with flirts was unbecoming.

Marcus Wales wondered what Cora would think when she

found out Zebadiah was in the ground, buried by the very boy whom she made the most fun of.

Phony Landers woke to the sound of snow melting off the roof. He blinked at the sun that sliced through the corner of the window. Things were thawing already. He glanced at Joe Wood, a blanket pulled over his head, his body slack in sleep. Landers rose and pulled on his boots. After leaving the shed, he saw an axe leaning against a pole of the dog run, so he snatched it up. The wood pile was easy to find, its top piled white with snow, but the chopping block stood like a thing of granite, so he headed for it. He limbered up with a few empty strokes and then began attacking the stacked wood, one piece at a time, splitting each with a joyful vengeance.

The woman heard the noise and saw him through the window. *Let him work,* she thought. After a time, she saw him remove his coat and wage further war against the woodpile, the stack of chopped kindling growing. She took a frying pan down from its hook and began carving up thick ham slices. Every now and then she would steal a glance through the window. The crazy Mr. Landers was chopping enough wood to last a week. After a while, she could hear him stacking it along the wall in the dog run. When it grew silent, she opened the door and hollered for him to come into the house.

"Stomp your feet."

Landers obeyed, standing uncomfortably in the doorway.

"And close the door, please. You men are all alike."

"Much obliged, ma'am. I mean, for taking us in last night."

"My name is Mrs. Tallit. And you are welcome. Taking you in was not as messy as shooting you. I hate a mess."

She said this off-handedly, over her shoulder, but Phony could detect the humor in her voice. The glare of the snow was wearing off, and he could see that the little house was tidy as a pin, the meager furniture squared into its appointed place, curtains on the windows, with a hand-woven circle rug off to one side, bearing the cheerful colors of green and yellow. He looked for the boy, but then he saw the small loft in a dark recess, with a corner of a blanket hanging over the edge.

"How is your deputy?"

"Still asleep, I reckon. He's been on a chase and ran himself to a thin thread."

"That's an interesting way of putting it, Mr. Landers." She was busy in the small vestibule that served as her kitchen. The smell of cooking ham was the welcome evidence.

Phony saw the shelf of books then, and he fidgeted his way toward it. Six books, he counted. Worn but in decent condition. Spines of soft red, two of green, a brown, and a black. He leaned close to read the titles—*Eight Cousins. The Vicar of Bullhampton. The Three Musketeers.*

"You said you were a schoolteacher."

"Oh, well," he said, turning. He saw her standing in the opening between rooms, her apron showing small spots of grease. "I'm presently between jobs. But yes, I have done my time in a classroom. In fact, I served at a school very near to Plum Creek." He said this gesturing toward the book.

Mrs. Tallit nodded and then returned to her kitchen.

"You must be a reader," he said, loud enough for her to hear.

"I am. But those were my husband's books." She put down her potholder and came back into the room. She pointed to a framed photograph occupying the center of a small table by the hearth. Phony looked at it politely, studying the man, dark suit, white shirt, loose fitting back tie. There was a seriousness to the deep eyes, clean, whiskerless cheeks, turned down mouth. Handsome, though. Handsome enough for a woman as striking as Mrs. Tallit.

"Is he away?"

The woman nodded with what seemed ancient sorrow. "He's on the hill." She did not point. "Three years dead."

Phony Landers searched his mind for something to say, but

before he could form his words, she spoke again.

"I'll feed you first, Mr. Landers. If your deputy ever wakes up, he can eat cold ham and cold potatoes. Now come and sit. There's coffee."

The table was small, but she sat across from him and ate without embarrassment. There were eggs and bread too, and Landers put forth his best manners in eating without wolfing. Neither spoke for a while, until a knock came to the door. It was Wood, and he opened the door just wide enough to announce himself.

"Come inside," she ordered. "Your plate is on the stove."

Joe Wood was even more awkward in his clumsy entry. "I'm beholdin, ma'am."

"Well, you look a mite fitter than you did last night, Marshal."

The deputy shuffled his boots as if they were cast in lead. "You needn't have fixed breakfast for us."

"I make breakfast every day. I just made it bigger today. Thanks to Mr. Landers, here and his wood chopping skills, Kip gets to sleep up to milking time."

Joe Wood took in the room. He found it not altogether different from his own little house, except it had the definite touch of a woman. There were lacy things instead of leather wares, china dishes instead of tin plates, and handmade patch quilts instead of Indian blankets.

The woman was standing with his plate when Joe Wood saw the photograph. Phony Landers saw the deputy stiffen. The lawman took a step closer and then stepped away in obvious retreat.

"Com'on schoolteacher. We've gotta ride." Wood nearly stumbled backward as he said this, his face suddenly white.

"Your breakfast, Marshal. It's getting cold."

"Eat, Joe, before—"

Wood bellowed. "Git the horses. We gotta ride."

Phony and the woman shared confused glances.

"Much obliged, ma'am," Wood said, faltering toward the door. He flung it open and was through.

"Beats me, Mrs. Tallit. Beats me all to heck," Phony said,

searching his pocket for his wallet and fumbled out a pair of coins.

"Don't you insult me too, Mr. Landers. Keep your money."

"But…"

She held up her hand.

Behind them the boy Kip stirred. Phony and the woman looked at each other again. "It was truly a pleasure, Mrs. Tallit. I can only apologize for the deputy's boorish behavior." He looked into her face, saw the strained beauty of a once happier woman and felt the dangerous urge to touch her arm. If she did not need that physical touch, he certainly did. But he turned instead and left the house.

Wood was leading the horses from the barn, saddled and ready. They mounted wordlessly and left the yard without looking back. Phony's back was hunched in anger, and he rode two horse lengths behind so as not to be tempted to shoot the bastard.

After nearly an hour, Phony spoke. "What the hell was that all about?"

"None of yer business is what."

"You have a reason for be being such an ass?"

Wood didn't answer.

"Somewhere in Scripture we're told to care for orphans and widows. I reckon you plum thumbed your nose at both."

"Shut it, Landers."

"I'm not afraid of you, you uncouth cur."

The deputy reined in. Whipping his horse around, Wood sat facing the schoolteacher.

Landers was fuming. "All that woman did for us. And you—"

"I know who she is. She's Mrs. Tallit. Mrs. John Tallit. And if you say one more word to me about her, about her being a widow, or her damn breakfast, I'm going to tie you to a tree. Now show me where in the hell we are so we can catch up to Kammers."

Phony Landers was overcome by shock. He sat open-mouthed, trying to digest the deputy's strange outburst and put some meaning to it. But he knew it would require brainwork, and at this moment his brain had just gone numb.

Billows of steam rose from the gurgling, gray water of the hot springs, a misshaped circular pool resting inside a jagged clearing where a halo of scrub evergreens grew out of the hoary rocks. Snow covered the banks, and nearby, straining its own rickety frame, was an old sweat lodge, once used by Indians in the days of their roaming.

Erastus Kammers was cheered by this site, and he scrambled from his saddle and stood before the approaching women like a circus ringmaster introducing a great trapeze show. He spun on his heel, arms spread, laughing in boyish fashion. "Your deliverance from the cold, ladies. My compliments to you for your uncomplaining forbearance. Within minutes you shall be warmed to your very souls."

The girls drew their horses up to the lodge and stared down at the steaming circle of water. "I ain't getting in there," Cora said.

"Don't be so sure," Yelena countered. "Hazel needs something to warm her. We all do."

"I meant I ain't standing naked in front of these vultures," Cora said.

But even as they were talking, Elise slid off of her horse and tramped through the snow to the edge of the water. She could already feel its warmth just from the circling steam. Without a moment's hesitation, she pulled off her simple dress and, standing naked, stepped into the soothing tarn.

"Yahoo," cried Kammers. "That's the spirit."

"Good Lord," whispered Rose of Sharon. "That girl's gone crazy as a loon."

"Join in the fun, ladies. Don't be shy."

Toss Griffin, toothless Rufus Mead, and Frank King edged their horses closer and watched in lascivious gawking as the normally timid Elise sank to her neck. The young woman's brown hair seemed to shine like bronze against the gray water. She turned then and looked at the others, her hand coming up out of the water and dripping. It fluttered a birdlike greeting to all who stood watching, and then she was gone, down below the water's surface, a soft trail of bubbles rising.

It was Rose who understood the sickening wave of Elise's hand. Off her horse in a flash, Rose ran to the water's edge. An instant's hesitation and then she was in—boots, clothes and all—her arms searching beneath the leaden surface, her fingers grabbing eel-like. There were no clothes to grasp onto so Rose did the only thing left to her. Pulling in a big breath she went down. The warmth of the water helped her move swiftly, smoothly. There beneath, in forced fetal position against the dark rocks, her long hair floating around her face, the perfect picture of a mermaid, was Elise. For one brief moment, their eyes met underwater, and something both beautiful and horrible passed between them.

They broke the surface together, Rose's fingers still entwined in Elise's tangled, wet hair. Yelena was standing close on the shore, holding Elise's dress so to cover the near-drowned girl. Rose half dragged her to the shore, and quickly the dress was wrapped around her. Kammers' men, and Kammers himself, stood in stupid wonder at the spectacle that had just unfolded before their eyes. When Rose came out of the pool, her boots filled with water, her clothes dripping gutters of water, Kammers began to clap. He started out clapping slowly, but then increased it, and soon the other outlaws joined in. "Excellent performance, ladies. Bravo," Kammers howled with glee.

As Yelena helped the now covered Elise to the Indian hut, it was young Hazel who came to Rose and helped her from the pool. But Cora, her fury rising, searched the rocky shoreline until she found what she wanted. A perfectly smooth stone, the size of a quail egg. She picked it up, and in one fluid motion heaved it at Erastus Kammers. The stone hit him on the shoulder, but before the outlaw realized what had happened, another one struck him on the cheek. She hit him two more times before Kammers was on her, and in one wrenching twist of her arm, he shoved her to the water's edge and pushed her in. She landed with a splash, sputtering like a hen. When she cleared her face of water and hair, she found herself staring into the killing end of Kammers' Colt.

"You are becoming more trouble than you are worth, girl." The pistol roared and a bullet struck the water inches from her. He fired again, another bullet, whistling past her head. He walked into the water himself now and placed the pistol against Cora's forehead. The hammer clicked back again. He waited. Without turning he hollered out, "Whaddya think, Frank King?"

King sat coolly in his saddle. "She's nothing to me. This is your harem, not mine. But..."

Kammers looked into Cora's eyes, and he saw for the first time something that had moved beyond her hatred and her fury. It was fear.

"But what, Frank? But what?"

"Well, I was just thinking. I'd hate to see this lovely pool all littered with her brains before I had a chance to enjoy its healing powers." He laughed. "Besides, Kammers, she *is* awful damn pretty."

Kammers hesitated. He detected a slight quiver to Cora's bottom lip, and it gave him a terrifying strength. It was a harming strength, a supremacy that had often ended in a lust for blood. He moved the pistol down and caressed Cora's cheek with the Colt's long barrel. He moved it upward then and fired. Cora jerked, the thunder deafening, the bullet passing harmless into the water behind her.

The outlaw leader gripped Cora by the wrist and shoved her toward the shore. "Out, damned spot! Out, I say!" Turning abruptly then, Kammers looked at Frank King. "Come and claim your prize. She's yours to do as you see fit."

Chapter 11

BOONE CROWE DID NOT talk about the Wilderness, or Spotsylvania, because to speak of it was to invite it into his dreams, and that nightmare tangle of death was a thing best left undisturbed. Commanding his company into that black welter of tripping underbrush, of roots and vines, of muddling thickets, slapping branches and ghostly images of devils and demons—became a thing of deadly wonder. General Hancock, crossing the Orange Turnpike, put his boys into the face of the furnace. They fought hard for that scratch of forest, a sweltering, smoke-filled boiler of trees and shadows, of ghastly death and outlandish suffering.

And yet it was there again, something nagging in the back of his mind. It came finally, like the blossoming of a black rose. Something the dying Lampy Dixson had whispered. *Who's riding with Kammers?* Crowe'd asked. *Nobody to fret about*, the outlaw had said, coughing through his blood. *'Cept Mr. Smoot.* Smoot. Hancock had spoken that name repeatedly to his officers the night before battle. *Keep General Smoot's cavalry from flanking us.* Smoot's cavalry. *If Smoot gets between us and the left, there'll be hell to pay.* Crowe considered now, through an almost Biblical revelation, who the real leader of this crazed bunch was. It was Smoot. It had to be. An old war horse, like himself. Crafty as a black adder. Quiet and calculating.

Boone Crowe watched the trail twist and turn ahead, up through the canyon walls, the warming wind already melting the snow. But his mind was on Smoot. Kammers, he realized now, was merely the actor on the stage, an unstable son of the Lost Cause, a charmed relic of a failed antebellum fantasy. The director of this grand play though was Smoot. *Why the hell did all those crazies end up in Wyoming Territory?* He wondered this with bitter frustration.

Noting Crowe's silence, Giles Roman edged his bay alongside the marshal's Ghost Horse. "You sensing trouble?"

87

"Not yet. But it's coming," he said, without turning to look at the boy. They had been traveling fast, without stops, but now, pointing with a gloved hand, Crowe said, "There, in that cleft. See it?"

Roman tensed, looking. "By them scrub trees?"

Boone Crowe did not answer; instead; he rode directly to it, circling his horse around a gang of boulders that were strewn to the side of the trail, and which revealed a cave-like cove beneath the dry pines. On the ground, lying like a wounded bird, was a woman's scarf, brown and yellow and limp. It laid fluttering against the lee of one of the boulders, nestled at the base like a breathless crier.

The young Roman saw it too now, and after dismounting quickly, he ran to it. Bending, he lifted the scarf and shook leafy snow from it. He held it up to the marshal, but neither spoke. The lawman dismounted, and together they searched the area. There was no sign of a camp, so the scarf had *not* been left there by accident; it was dropped intentionally.

"This clears up any doubts we might have had. They're up there," Crowe said. He studied the place where they stood, entering the canopy of pine branches that created the sheltering cove. "We have to think this out. Wouldn't be wise ridin into the thick of 'em. Not with them women amongst 'em."

"What you figure?"

Crowe studied the sun, his gloved hand stroking his chin whiskers. "I figure this. We're close. It's in the very air around us." He wove his arm in a circular motion. "There's good cover here. A good defensive position in case they decide to give us another charge. So, this here will be a base camp of sorts. May as well settle in this cove."

"Whaddya mean, it's in the air?"

"War talk, Roman. The enemy always carries a smell. Not a smell you get with yer nose. You get it in yer bones. A heaviness in the air that tells you what yer eyes and ears can't. Trackers have it. Scouts too. You come to sense the enemy before you see 'em."

Roman could only nod in queer admiration.

"I heard a'that place," Toss Griffin said.

Rufus Mead said it again. "Andersonville." He spoke the word as if spitting poison off his tongue. "Lost the whole bunch in that scurvy-bitten place. First my grinders then my canines. My front ones was last to go. Hangin on to the last." He ran a finger across his gums to illustrate.

The two sat side-by-side with their backs against a cluster of rocks. Their bodies were clean from their naked bathing, but they had returned to the stale clothes they had been wearing. Earlier they had watched the last of the girls ease into the pool fully clothed, the quiet Yelena and the child, Hazel. Toss was wondering what it would be like to have for himself a gal as pretty as this Yelena. He wondered further how in hell he got mixed up with this outfit in the first place and ending up on the wrong side of love. His face still bore the claw marks of the witch girl, Cora. And, in spite of her dunking, she still had a claim to his sombrero. But Kammers had shaken the pepper out of that one. Now she was Frank King's girl, leaving Toss free of the wildcat's annoyance. She was pretty, but he was no match for her.

"How'd you make it with Lampy then, you bein a Yank and he a Confederate?"

Rufus worked his jaw in reply. "Lampy was a guard at that hellhole. He took a likin to me on account I was no trouble to him. When old Grant finally got around to whipping Lee's ass, things got turned around. Then it were I who done the guardin. For a spell anyway. We was most too weak to do much guardin. But at least in idea, till all the Johnnies got sent home by Father Abe. We patched up our war differences and plum struck out together."

"You seemed pretty casual about leavin him out there by his own self," Toss said, recalling how he and Rufus and had turned tail and run.

"My heart's growed a mighty big callus 'cause of all the killin I've seen. We all got our time. Lampy chose his. I wasn't ready yet."

Toss thought about this for a minute. "What then about these womenfolk?"

"Them? Oh, they is supposed to me Kammers' playthings. Still might be. But I don't reckon he thought that out too well. They're provin a handful." He gave a grunting laugh.

"Well, I hope he's in a sharing mood," Toss said.

Wyoming had a great way of recovering herself from bad weather. Up on the flats the howling wind had erased the bulk of the snow, its warmth coming from a place where the sun shone, somewhere in the direction in which Marcus Wales was riding. He let his hat fall against his back, held there by a leather thong, with his full, curly hair twisting with the gusts and his face set like flint. His joy—that which he had—was in knowing that Utah was to his back. And that one day his pa would look far and wide for his return but would only be left wondering. He lulled astride his horse, his mind on his mission, that of rejoining the marshal and rescuing the girls. And then what? He didn't know yet. Being shot at and shooting back was one thing. But facing a girl's bewitchment was something altogether more fearsome.

It was the horse that baulked first. Looking ahead, into the flatness, he saw a lone Indian tipi stuck in the middle of nowhere, out of place as a cactus at the North Pole. He sat studying it for a long time, wondering at its purpose. It was 1884—rightly or wrongly, the Indians had been moved out. As he edged closer, he also saw one of those burial platforms that stood on stilts behind the tipi. He approached cautiously, noticing a passel of horse prints in the mucky ground, accompanied by boot heel marks.

Wales dismounted, keeping his horse between himself and the tipi. The wind was pulling at one of the buffalo hide flaps of the lodge's entrance, and he was able to see now that there was a strewn mess of objects littering the ground—shredded blankets, broken clay pots, and a dead dog. Seeing this Wales pulled one of Wilcox's revolvers from its sheath. The wind came whistling through the wooden burial stilts with an eerie howling moan, and it chilled him. Another noise was added to this, another mournful one, but this one not made by the wind.

Glancing over his shoulder, Wales studied the surrounding plains, making sure he wasn't being watched by some far-off pair of eyes. Something had happened here, but he wasn't sure just what. Stepping carefully around the tipi, he saw that one of the supporting columns was broken, and the burial platform was leaning at a severe slant. And then he saw the woman and heard her wailings.

Marcus Wales had learned a great deal about caution in these past days, and he was applying it now. His eyes kept darting to the distance slopes of landscape where an ambush might be in the making. He watched the tipi flap too, half expecting someone to burst forth with evil intent. Without realizing it, he had arrived to within five feet of the woman. She was ancient, he could see now, her hair the color of hammered steel. It fell loose at her shoulders, blowing wild in the wind. And before her, on the ground, was a blanket-wrapped body; the body that presumably belonged on the burial platform.

The woman had not heard his approach because of the wind and her own cries. Holstering his pistol, Wales eased around so his shadow fell upon her. She looked up suddenly, her deeply wrinkled face showing both horror and resolute surrender. She instantly threw herself upon the corpse and spread her arms in the form of protection.

Through his own puzzlement, the young man held up his hands, palms outward, hoping to show he meant no harm. He tried feeble forms of hand motions, motioning in gentle gestures toward the platform and then to the dead person. He spread his arm toward the strewn mess and the dead dog, and he saw that her eyes followed. So, very slowly, he moved closer and after a hesitation, he lowered himself to his knees in front of her beside the body. His youthful innocence must had shown itself as harmlessness, in spite of the two pistols at his hips, his curly hair and gentle eyes drawing her into his trust.

"Who…did…this?" His soft voice helped in his appeal.

The old woman blinked. She held up one finger on each hand.

"Two?" He remembered the heel marks in the mud. "Two men?" He tapped lightly against his chest and held up two of his own fingers. "Two men?"

She nodded.

"Did…did they kill him," Wales asked, touching the body.

She seemed to understand and shook her head. She motioned in a way to indicate he was already sleeping in death. But then she held up her two fingers again and pointed to the broken wood column. Turning to the strewn mess again, Wales held up his two fingers. The woman nodded.

Marcus Wales looked at the sky as if hoping to find some message written there, something that would help him understand exactly what happened here. What he surmised was that two men had come here, robbed what little she had, mocked the burial tradition of the woman, killed the dog, and rode off. The whole thing seemed ghastly, but knowing what Kammers had done, the young man was fast learning that living the farm life in Utah had sheltered him from a different world altogether—a world peopled by wicked men.

Hanging his pistol belt over the pummel of his saddle, Wales began repairing the platform's broken column. This took a half hour's work of refastening the splintered wood with straps of leather. Next he lifted the bundled body. It was light, and through further hand communication, he learned it was her aged husband, an old Shoshone warrior turned beggar out of necessity. Struggling on a rickety ladder, he managed to return the old warrior to his appropriate resting place.

Wales buried the dog using a fossilized buffalo hip bone to

dig with, a utensil that the old woman had possessed and used most of her life. He watched as she gathered up her scattered belongings. *What's going to happen to her now?* he wondered. He can't very well leave her here alone. Or could he? In reality, and judging from her history, she was probably tougher than he was. She was born tougher and had lived through many heartaches, personal and those delivered to her people. But eventually more bad men would come. Men, born with fiends' hearts, who prey on the weak.

Daylight was ebbing. He'd been fooled by the time, so he reluctantly made a camp under the only tree in sight, a sad-looking elm that rooted itself fifty yards from the burial podium. It would be the second time he slept next to a dead man, and he hoped it did not become a habit. After he had attended to the horses and built a small fire of damp, smoky tinder, the old woman hobbled out of her tipi and brought him a bowl of pemmican. Her gray eyes were deep with history. She touched him on the head and left.

Mr. Smoot saw the two riders coming from a long ways off. He had been watching the back trail for a full day now, moving here and there, exploring the landscape with a proficiency adapted from his war days. The chiseled canyons of Kammers' camp were a half-day's ride away, and with night coming on, Mr. Smoot knew he would be out on this scout for a while longer. *All in the name of prudence*, he thought. And here, like manna from heaven, came two riders.

The riders were coming across an open plain, heading in the direction of the Kitty Hart. They had to be, since there was no other sensible reason to be out here in the middle of this Wyoming backcountry. There was purpose in their gait, and even from this distance, the old general, who knew horses and men, saw power in the man on the right. *Lawman*, he judged. *Well, come on then.*

Mr. Smoot assumed they had seen him too, or seen his horse, as like the riders, he was exposed to the wide open vista. But that mattered not. He moved to his horse and pulled his rifle from its scabbard. It was a Winchester 1873 .44–40, with its long, sleek barrel and the promise of a long-range capacity to go with it. He steadied his horse, and after placing the barrel of the rifle across the belly of the saddle delicately, he sighted in on the rider on the right. His horse was used to these antics, so he did not fear a misfire. A soft hum came from deep inside him and drawing one last breath, he held it and gently squeezed the trigger.

Mr. Smoot's horse only shivered, as if chasing off a horsefly, and the outlaw watched as the right-hand rider left his saddle as if pulled by a rope. The man's horse leapt, stung by the falling man's spurs. The other man, finally hearing the echoing crack of the Winchester, spun out of his saddle, looking first at the fallen man and then upward, across the flat plane of land to where the smoke and fire of Mr. Smoot's second shot flashed. A horse dropped onto its front knees and then over onto its side, dead. Hesitating only a moment, the second man threw himself behind this dead horse for shelter.

The old general waited, amused. He watched the man behind the horse fumble with the rigging of the dead animal. A long pause and then suddenly a return burst of fire and the unmistakable roar of a Sharps threw a flat echo through the thin air. The heavy slug struck the ground beneath Mr. Smoot's horse causing it to dance.

"What in hell?" *Not here, not now*, he thought. Finding the stirrup, Mr. Smoot jockeyed himself into the saddle and made a race of getting away from the Sharps. He'd seen that wicked thing take a man's whole arm off. Or gut a horse. And he wasn't in the mood to be horseless out here. *I got me one*, he thought. It would be good enough. And it should take the spirit out of the second one.

Ahead stretched darkness and he rode into it.

Joe Wood lay on his back with his eyes open. He was not dead, not yet, but his chest showed a spreading stain of red-black blood. Phony Landers laid the Sharps across the dead horse and knelt at Wood's side.

"Am…am I…"

"Don't talk."

"Who was…he…?"

"I don't know. Be still so I can look you over."

Wood tried to rise up onto one side, but Phony Landers would have none of it. He grabbed Wood's face between his thumb and palm. "Listen, you stupid lawman. Lay still. I don't feel like digging your grave." They stared deeply into each other's eyes, and Landers could see the glassy gaze of shock setting in.

The deputy lay back down, his breathing rapid and broken. The Winchester slug had punched a hole in his upper right chest, away from his heart but close to his lung. Landers let his hand creep beneath Wood's back, feeling for an exit wound, and his finger found a blown out chunk of flesh and bone, his hand coming away slick with blood. *Could be a good thing*, he thought. *Maybe.* He didn't really know for sure. He'd never seen a man shot through like this before. It was the bleeding he needed to stop. That much he knew. And the ground was cold and wet.

Landers looked at the dead horse as if he might speak to him. Everywhere the blue stem rippled in the wind, and he looked again to where the man had fired his rifle from. *What if he comes back?* Landers went to Wood's dead horse and pulled back the flap on the saddlebags. Inside were cartridges for the Sharps, a waxed bag of jerked meat, and corndodgers. Digging to the bottom he found a shirt.

After he ripped the shirt in two, Landers applied one wad of the shirt to Wood's chest and the other he put into the exit hole. Next, he retrieved one of his own spare shirts, and using the cut reins from the dead horse, he used the leather to tie the fabric patches tight to both front and back. Throughout this he watched the hill before him, listening for any sound that might mean the return of the shooter.

"Joe. Listen, we've gotta get out of here. And that means getting you back on a horse."

Joe Wood grunted.

"I'll not lie. It might kill you to move you. But if we don't leave this place, you'll die anyway."

Moving with painstaking caution, Landers helped the deputy onto his feet. Lander's horse seemed spooked at first, but the schoolteacher's soothing voice steadied it, and he carefully eased Wood up and onto the saddle. Once he was on the horse, the wounded man folded over the pummel, his arms hanging as if passed out. Or dead. Landers touched the side of Wood's face. "Don't leave me now, Joe. We're just going back to that creek we passed. Two miles. Hang on."

Phony Landers took up the reins of his horse then, and with the deputy's saddlebags over his shoulder and the Sharps in his other hand, he hastened on foot into the mysterious, dark calamity of life and death.

Chapter 12

THE MOON THREW A picket-fence pattern onto the dirt floor of the sweat lodge. Blood-orange embers glowed from a rocked in circle of coals. Huddled around the fire's warmth the five young women shivered inside their damp clothes. Hazel's head kept bobbing from exhaustion, but she had reached the point where she refused to sleep, a mixture of fear and defensiveness. Yelena brushed the girl's yellow hair with her fingers, pulling through the long strands.

Cora sat in deep silence, her face empty of its usual spirit. Rose of Sharon, her medicine bag open, was mixing a dressing of crushed oats and applying it to Cora's wrist where Kammers had torn the skin when manhandling her. She had applied nettle dust, used for larger wounds, but wanted her to heal quickly. Rose studied the girl as she worked, aware of her uncharacteristic withdrawal. "Found your match, did you?"

The girl only blinked.

"I'm glad it was Kammers who gave you that lesson." Her words were not cruel, only truthful. She spoke in soft, clipped sentences, her smoky voice portraying urgency. "You set yourself up for that. Now you can hate him. And you don't have to hate me. I figured that job was going to fall on me. Now it's done." She let her words sink in.

Cora's eyes moved to meet Rose's, so the older woman knew she was listening, but even past the hollow stare of defeat, there still flickered in Cora a spark of dislike for the lecture, and for the woman delivering it.

"Being tough's a fine thing. Especially in this country. A woman needs it. But there is a difference. Being tough is not the same as being headstrong. I have tried many times to show you easier ways to do things. You resisted me at every turn."

Even in the dim light of the lodge, Rose could see the tears balancing on the rims of Cora's eyes. In a second, they spilled down her cheeks.

"Listen, sister," Rose went on, "I've lived in the emptiness of Utah a long time. Long enough. Now I know…I don't want to go back. But I had to survive. I came out just like you did. And as much as we might have despised Hester, I learned from her. See this." Rose tapped her chest. "I have a rebel's heart too. Just like you. The difference? I know when to pick my battles."

Cora wiped at her face, her eyes on the ground now.

"You want to get out of here alive? Being bull-headed isn't the way. Socking two-bit cowpunchers isn't the way. Throwing rocks at a killer isn't the way." Rose reached over and with a gentle hand lifted Cora's chin. "For the first time in your life, girl, you better start listening to your elders." Her voice was husky with passion.

Cora wanted to jerk her head away, but sensibly refrained. Zebadiah would come for her. She knew it. He would not fail her. She knew he would go to the ends of the earth to be with her now…*now* that she was free of Prescott.

Elise, who had been listening, touched Rose's sleeve. "I'm sorry for what I did. *I'm*…not crazy. Really. I was…just *scared*."

Rose gave her a tender look. "We're all scared, Elise."

Like a ghost in the night, Mr. Smoot slipped into the camp. Frank King was sitting alone near the warm, moon-silvered water of the springs. Rufus Mead and Toss Griffin came out of their sleep and watched the graybeard tend to his horse in the darkness. They studied him, his steady movements, his poised bearing, and they wondered. Rufus knew about his generalship but little more. He pondered about whether he'd ever faced him in battle. With Lampy gone now, the toothless hobo was beginning, in his quiet moments, to relive the war. The war, and his loyalties. What the hell was he doing here?

Toss lay back down, and in a minute, the soft purring of his sleep ruffled around him. *And this kid*, Rufus thought. An out-of-work cowboy making bad decisions. He'd make a bet, if he had someone to make a bet with—this boy Toss would be dead before the week was out. He'd seen it a hundred times before. He saw it a dozen times at Gettysburg alone. Men shoving letters into his hands. Or just plain shadows passing over their faces. The devil's shadow, telling them they would not see tomorrow. And at Andersonville. Alive one day, dead the next. If it wasn't the raiders, or scurvy, it was the flying away of all hope. That was the big killer. Hopelessness. Always has been.

Rufus Mead cursed Lampy Dixson now for ever befriending him. And he cursed himself for being so empty after the war that he lost all sight of loyalty. *What the hell am I doing here?* he thought again.

"I put a crimp in that posse, Colonel," Mr. Smoot said.

Kammers sat up, the battered copy of *Macbeth* falling from his lap. He picked it up and looked at his scout. "Tell me."

"Just as I figured. They were coming across the flats. Hoping to flank us up topside. I put one down and killed his horse. The other man with him. Well, I figure he lost his appetite for the chase." He did not mention the return fire, the rumble of the Sharps, and the fear it put in him.

Kammers listened, his gaze drifting into the spume of the shiny pool. His eyes found King sitting sleepless in the moon glow. "'Fire burn, and cauldron bubble.'"

"Excuse me?"

"Swan Collinear. My sister's friend. I've kept her face hidden in my heart all these years. Inside her eyes shone the stars of the southern heavens. And she *was* a swan, Mr. Smoot. Her skin white as a flower. She drove lightning bolts into my sleep. My desire for her made me cry like a suckling. *Hallo Master Erastus*, she would say. *Aren't you the little gentleman?* Her laugh dripped honey. And I hated her in my love."

Mr. Smoot remained silent. A scent of sulfur emitted from Kammers' madness, and the scout turned away.

"And there sits the betrayer."

Mr. Smoot didn't need to look to know who Kammers' meant. Frank King sat on his own throne. *Two dueling kings*, Mr. Smoot remembered. He too knew *Macbeth*.

"A Confederate officer came one day," Kammers rambled on. "He sat on the veranda with my father, and they spoke of battle. Captain Hampton Cleve was the man's name. His arm was in a sling. From a wound. At Grimball's Landing."

Kammers stood and his arm swept toward the star-filled sky. "It was high summer. The girls were out, blossoming like the flowers. War was close, but it had not touched us. Not yet. Not then. There were other officers there too. The darkies had been ordered to dress the lawn with tables for an afternoon supper. I can see the tables yet. The kitchen girls, Patty and Selfish, produced bowls of cobbed corn, okra, and breaded catfish. Melons and cakes and collard greens and yams. And hams the size of a horse's head."

Mr. Smoot thought he saw Kammers teeter a bit and wondered if he were drunk on top of his lunacy.

"Will all great Neptune's ocean wash this blood clean from my hand?"

Frank King, in his silence, was listening too. Mr. Smoot could see the leering twist on his lips. He waited. Finally, Kammers did stumble, but righted himself, straightening the front of his coat.

"They were in the big barn," he said. "Standing in a circle of light from through the rafters. He…this captain. And my Swan. And *they*…they were kissing." Pain etched deeply into his words. "I hid. And I watched them. He unfastened his saber, and his pistol belt. Swan lay down in the straw and…" Kammers leaned too far back and nearly toppled over. "And…do you know what she did, Mr. Smoot?"

The scout made no sound.

"She lifted her petticoats. That's what she did. She lifted them so that the captain could…"

Kammers sat down in the same spot he'd risen from. He put a hand in front of him, staring, as if it were some strange new instrument. "She was naked when I found her. And I looked at her. And she looked at me. Her skin was white as an oleander blossom."

"What did you do?" It was Frank King's voice coming across the silver water.

Kammers lifted his head, startled out of his vision. "Why, I did the only thing I could do. The captain. He had left his saber. So…so I killed her. I put the saber between her naked breasts and…"

Mr. Smoot felt bile rise in his throat. He glanced at King and saw the man's smirk widen.

Kammers was still looking at his hand. "All the perfumes of Arabia will not sweeten this little hand."

Mud birds rattled through the branches of the ill-shaped trees along the creek. Joe Wood, lost in delirium, lay covered in a bedroll on a grassy patch of the stream's bank. Only in a dream world did the noise of hacking and breaking of branches reach him. In the dark, Phony Landers was at work constructing a makeshift travois. He managed, through a long night of labor, to secure the two supporting poles. He used more of the leather from the dead horse's bridle to bind the pieces together.

Saddle blankets stretched across the frame and knotted with anything Landers could find to brace it up provided the bed that he would place Wood on at first light. He knew where he had to go. There was no place else to go—Mrs. Tallit's. He went to the creek and washed the work from his hands. He removed his hat and threw water on his face. The moon threw a long streak of silver down the middle of the water and Phony took a moment to search for his reflection. The blur of his face, stretched and distorted by the snow-melted current, was that of a stranger. The ambush of Joe Wood put a weird twist in his former self. He had never in his life concerned himself with anything but taking care of his own needs. No longer. But stranger still, beyond needing to keep the deputy alive, was an acidy aftertaste to the shooting. It was anger. And it was a desire for revenge. He didn't know if he liked that. Snatching up a twig, he brushed away his reflection.

A string of incomprehensible utterances floated up from Woods. Phony went to him and studied his face in the moonlight. His eyes were closed, but his face twisted with pain and confusion. Landers decided to take a chance.

"Joe, I'm taking you to Mrs. Tallit's farm."

The deputy's expression darkened, and his eyes opened into narrow slits. "No. Not..."

"There's no place else."

Wood shook his head. "You can't."

"What happened? Tell me."

A long time passed, and Landers figured the wounded man had fallen asleep. But after a while, Wood's eyes opened again, and he stared angrily at his tormenter. "I killed her husband."

Landers tried to cover his shock. He briefly put a hand over his own face as if to mask the image. "When?" he said, finally. "When did you kill her husband?"

Wood's voice was weak, and Landers feared this talking might use up the last of his strength. "*Three*...three years."

"Was he a bad man?"

The deputy shook his head. "I...killed the *wrong* man."

"Did you know she was his wife when we stopped there?"

Wood tried to lift his hand to his face, but he was too weak. "Saw the tintype. Saw his face. It was...*him*."

"That's why you wanted to get outta there. She didn't know?" Landers sat back and considered this. *This changes things*, he thought. He stared into the creek water. *Or does it?*

As the long night faded and a faint prairie dawn opened pink

102

on the horizon, Phony Landers heard the whole story. Deputy Wood was on the trail of escaped prisoner Othello Hardy. In his flight, Hardy had stolen a prized thoroughbred racer from Bishop Elgin Prescott. As the pieces came together, it was later determined that Hardy made it to Fort Tillman where he left the horse with the liveryman with instructions to keep it or sell as he saw fit. Then Othello Hardy jumped an eastbound train and disappeared. John Tallit, who was in Fort Tillman, saw the fine animal and inquired about it. Within minutes the exchange was made, and Tallit headed for home with his new horse, no doubt reveling in his good fortune.

Prescott had given Wood a description of his coveted beauty, relating in great detail each marking that the horse possessed. *She's one in a million*, Prescott had said. *You can't miss her.* And Wood did not miss her. He came upon the horse and Tallit's campfire, thinking he had finally caught up to Hardy. When Tallit reached in his coat pocket to produce the bill of sale, Wood thought he was going for a gun, and the deputy shot him dead. Wood, realizing his mistake, fled like a bad man himself. He quit his marshaling job and became a recluse on his remote ranch.

Some unemployed cowboys found the body, knew where he lived, and took John Tallit to his wife. End of story. Until Erastus Kammers made his own escape from the same New Mexican prison Hardy had escaped from. Kammers, with a different purpose altogether, made straight for Prescott's ranch, not for horses, but for women. When Boone Crowe showed up with the story, it was Joe Wood's hope that Kammers could lead him to Othello Hardy.

The whole nightmare of the snowstorm was behind them, eradicated by the warm wind. The schoolteacher eased his ward onto the travois and covered him with a saddle blanket. Then after Landers climbed into the saddle, the travois poles fastened awkwardly around him, he and Wood set out for the farm of the widow Tallit.

Chapter 13

Sleep evaded Marshal Boone Crowe. The stitch in his side from his wound in the Wilderness, and the Ute arrow that had pierced him in the same place only last year, seemed to speak to him in returning agony. A cavalryman without a horse, he found himself afoot in the knotted tangle of roots and severed limbs inside the smoky woods, fires burning and bullets singing and thudding into trees and bodies, the mess of their bloated bulks scattered like granite works.

Eva, had she lived, might have brushed back these memories with the softness of her voice. Or the mere subtlety of her presence. Did women possess such powers? Did they own secrets in their womanhood, unexplainable, that might remake the wounded and scarred man? He feared he would never know. Up this very canyon were five women. Some but girls still. Because of Eva, he wanted desperately to save them. Save them from what he had not been able to save Eva.

Earlier, while Roman tended to the horses, Crowe had walked up through the narrow gorge looking for signs and to study the lay of the land. This was new country to him. Wyoming was too big for him to have seen it all, though he had seen much of it. A mile up he saw where the ravine turned a corner and there, on the ground, just like the abandoned scarf, was a piece of torn garment, a ripped triangle of white lying along the loose gravel of the trail. He pocketed it, stared ahead into the growing darkness, and then returned to the camp.

It had been the brilliant silence of the deep night that had troubled his mind, but now, as a grain of dawn filtered down through the arroyos, he fought off his weariness with coffee as black as coal dust. The plan he had been working up in his mind all night was still not a thing completed. He wished he had Tugs Bigelow with him. Bigelow and his sharpshooter's eye. If he could disable them before they broke out onto level ground, it could encourage a surrender. But Tugs Bigelow was a couple hundred miles away, chasing horses up by Sheridan. As for his deputy, Rud Lacrosse, it was just as well he wasn't here. This was no place for a lovesick lawman. What he had was Giles Roman, a mostly untested farm boy. A boy he had taken a liking too.

That was always the trouble.

The old Indian woman had waved him on, so Marcus Wales reluctantly left her alone, standing in the wind beneath the death platform of her husband. He headed toward the open land that lead toward the mountains and the place where he hoped to find Boone Crowe and Giles Roman. Several times he crossed the tracks of the two men who had harassed the Indian woman the day before, but he kept on his steady pace, due northwest.

A sensation of great mystery passed through him as he pondered the image of his former self. Shame covered him when he saw how timid he had been, how easily belittled he was. It seemed centuries ago—not mere days—when he could be so easily cowed, by boy and girl alike. *Is it the pistols?* he wondered. No. It was more. Marshal Crowe had sent him home because he feared for his life. But it took a violent storm and the mocking, dead Wilcox and the hateful voice of his father—a voice he no longer hoped to hear—altogether that had sobered him. It was these things that gave him his life back. But there was one more thing, bigger. It had crept into his thoughts like a spider spinning its web—*he no longer feared death*. If he died doing this thing, then his life, and his death, would at least have amounted to something.

He dipped over the rim of a shallow cut in the prairie, and suddenly, there they were. Camp smoke rose from a small fire, and one man was bent over it working with breakfast fixings. The other man still laid in his bedding. Wales pulled up. It was them. The man on the ground was covered in an Indian blanket, a twin to the one the old woman had described.

The man at the fire looked up, and Wales stiffened. Twenty-five yards separated them. Standing, the man picked up a rifle that was propped against a saddle and turned, staring at Wales. The young man thought of the old woman he had helped and saw again the broken column and the body of the ancient warrior who had fallen to the ground. The woman's dry tears. The dead dog. He nudged his horse closer.

The man at the fire tipped his head slightly in an unfriendly greeting. "Mornin's full of surprises."

Wales did not speak, only looked the outfit over. They were tramps, plain enough. Wherever they camped, Wales was sure they left their trash behind. It showed in their unkempt beards and grease-smeared clothes.

"Roady, wake up. We got us some company."

The man in the bedding rolled over and looked up. He blinked. "Who the hell're you?"

The words in Wales head found their way out his mouth. "Where'd you get that blanket?"

"Huh?" The rifle came up level.

"The blanket. Who'd you steal it from?"

The man on the ground threw the blanket to the side. Wales saw that the man's holstered pistol was resting on the ground five feet away.

"I seen what you did to the old woman."

The man with the rifle put his head back as if to laugh, but no laugh came forth. "That old squaw. What's she to you?"

Wales allowed his anger to fight down his fear. This was bad. He'd stumbled into it without time to think it through. Without time to avoid it. Now, here he was. The next minute would tell the tale. It would write itself into his history. He heard a clock ticking in his head.

"You're mixin in where you're not wanted, sonny."

The horse's reins were knotted on the end, so Wales hooked them over the pummel in order to free his hands. They were shaking, so he clenched and unclenched his fists to calm them.

Suddenly, the man in his bedding rolled, his hand reaching for his pistol. Both of Wales' mismatched Colts came out of their sheaths, heavy and awkward in his hands. The man with the rifle shot from his hip, and the bullet sizzled by Wales' ear, waspy and hot. The left-handed Colt bucked, the force of its fire causing it to jump from his grip. It fell to the ground. The man with the rifle stiffened abruptly and then staggered backward. Wales realized he'd shot him.

The other man had retrieved his pistol, and after turning his body fully around, he shot twice. But Wales' horse had bolted backward, and both shots went wild. The horse spun, and bending over the pummel, Wales heard a third missed shot zing by. As his mount came full circle, Wales lifted his right-handed pistol, gripping it tightly, and with hammer back, he fired a .45 slug into the man's belly.

Dropping his pistol, the shot man grabbed at his middle, a shriek of pain piercing the gun smoke. Wales controlled his horse, his eyes on both men. Then, after dismounting, he nearly fell on shaky legs. The dropped Colt was on the ground before him, and he came to his knees to pick it up. The rifleman was trying to right himself, but blood seeping from his hip made his movements awkward. For a moment's worth of eternity, their eyes locked and deep hatred passed between them. Both of Wales' Colts thundered and bucked, once, twice, three times. When finally he could focus, he saw the rifleman spread out on the ground, mouth open in death.

The gut-shot man maintained his howling. The smell of powder burned in Wales' nostrils, and standing up slowly, he realized this whole thing has lasted but mere seconds. His hands were shaking mightily now. Holstering his left pistol, he walked cautiously to the man, who was sitting up, his legs outstretched in front of him, blood leaking through his fingers where he had them pressed to his stomach.

Wales felt lightheaded. The man looked up at him. He was

crying openly now. Wales wished the old woman had come with him so she could see this. So she would know that the men who had harmed her were dead and dying. But there was no bravado in him, only a relief that he was still alive himself. And that the Shoshone woman had been avenged.

Ignoring the dying man, Wales inspected the filthy camp. He picked up the rifleman's Winchester and then inspected the saddlebags for more shells. The scabbard that held the rifle lay amongst the saddles, and so Wales spent ten minutes lashing it to his own horse that stood still now, nostrils still flared. He did this not only because he wanted the weapon but also to help steady his nerves, his fingers trembling the whole time. He pushed the Winchester down into its casing across the saddle from his shot-gun and then turned back to the wounded man. It had not even occurred to him that the shotgun might have been a better choice than his pistols.

No words had been spoken between Wales and the man called Roady. He saw that the blood flow had increased, and the man had slumped over onto his side.

"God is waiting for your confession, mister," Marcus Wales finally said.

The man groaned.

"The old Indian woman. If I ever see her again, I'll tell her how poorly you died."

The two horses were worn out with broken hooves, so after cutting them loose, Wales left them. For a while, they followed, but after a couple of miles they stopped and watched the young man ride on, away from the rising sun.

The women were asleep. All except Elise. She silently crept from her place by the fire's weak embers and maneuvered through the lodge's dim, rickety interior to the reedy doorway. Peering out, she squinted into the gray dawn. A thin mist rose from the pool casting an ominous shadow across the campsite. Through the fog she could make out the old man Rufus, slumped in sleep near the rope corral where the horses stood in passive silence. Farther, against a cluster of rocks, the Griffin cowboy sat, chin against his chest, snoring. Kammers and the others were lost in the mist.

Barefooted, Elise edged out of the lodge, and taking small, noiseless steps, she worked her way past Rufus and beyond to the horses. Cora's Stella raised her head and shook a nod. Elise lifted the rope and moved in amongst them. They knew her, so they did not stamp. The horse she had been riding gave her a loving nudge. Grabbing the horse's forelock, she led it to the rope and lifted it, steering the horse out.

Rufus Mead came out of his sleep and looked around. He saw the girl. He watched as she put her fingers in the horse's mane and pull herself a'mount. He made no sound, and for a brief second their eyes met. His head lifted then, and he jerked his chin in the direction of down canyon. In an instant she was gone.

The sound of horse hoofs on shale brought the camp to life. Kammers flew out of the fog as if one of Shakespeare's ghosts. He saw the back end of the horse descending down through the canyon trail. In a rage he pushed Rufus aside, and pulling his Remington from his holster, Kammers emptied the pistol at the escaping form.

The women clambered out of the lodge. *Elise*, Rose of Sharon realized. She turned on Kammers and rushed at him just as he was firing his last shot. He pushed her aside, and she fell. Yelena came behind, and this time Kammers was caught unguarded, and the young woman brushed him to the ground. Enraged, Kammers leveled the pistol at Yelena and pulled the trigger, but the hammer landed on an empty chamber. He clicked it again and again, but all his bullets had been spent. Rising to his feet, he stormed toward Rufus, trying to reach for his pistol, but the old toothless soldier fended him off.

"You ain't usin my pistol to kill no woman," he mumbled.

Frank King and Toss Griffin were on the scene now. Kammers spun on them. "Give me your gun," he demanded. King and Griffin made no move.

Rose got to her feet. She moved to Yelena, and together they watched Kammers unravel. Finally, Mr. Smoot appeared. He looked at Kammers. "It's over, Colonel. Let it pass." Every eye watched as Kammers seemed to shrink from the command, the steam slowly leaving his rage like the hissing of a cooling engine, like the hot springs itself.

Erastus Kammers' second fired bullet had entered the back of Elise's right leg exactly where the knee bends, and it exited taking the knee cap with it. She felt the punch and cried out but held on, leaning over the horse's neck.

Down below Boone Crowe and Giles Roman heard the distant thunder of gunfire as it echoed down through the gorge. Scrambling out of their bedrolls and into the leaden dawn, they stood looking up into the twisting gorge. Roman glanced at the marshal but said nothing. The firing had also scattered a large group of geese from a place far above, and they filled the air now with their honking, their dark, bullet-bodies and long bottle necks drew the two men's eyes away. Suddenly, beneath this clatter, Roman grabbed Crowe's arm. "Listen," he said. "I hear a horse."

Down the canyon she rode, breakneck now, crazed with pain, her right leg limp as a rag. And still she hung on. The horse twisted through the rifts and breaks of the trail, tiring now, panting heavily. Elise finally looked up and saw, but not believing, the shadows of two men, arms open wide as if in greeting. She swallowed down a bitter cry, thinking they were more of Kammers' men. The horse saw them too, and as it tried to turn back, it reared instead, and Elise felt herself slipping from its back. But instead of falling onto the ground, she felt a man's arms wrap around her.

Roman clutched her, and her very weight nearly put him on

his back. But he held firm and cradled the girl tight around the waist. As he held her, he felt blood against his pant leg and the swinging pendulum of her useless leg. He had not even looked into her face yet, did not even know which of the girls she was. Crowe managed to stop the panicked horse and was moving it backward to steady it. Staring into the horse's crazed eyes, he spoke softly. He touched the horse's muzzle and held it affectionately.

Carrying the girl into the cove of trees where the two men had slept, Roman laid her down. It was now when he was able to see her face that he recognized her. Her eyes were pinched tight in pain, and Roman feared she had died. Boone was behind him now, and together they looked at the destroyed leg. Crowe shook his head.

"You know her?"

Roman nodded. "Elise."

At the sound of her name, she opened her eyes, and they darted back and forth like a captured bird.

"Are they close?" Crowe asked the girl this.

She grimaced a nod.

"The other girls? Are they alive?"

Again, she nodded.

Roman left and then returned with a canteen. He tipped it slowly to the girl's mouth and let her drink, the bulk of it running down her cheeks and chin. Her body began shaking violently. "Get a fire up," Crowe said. He stood then and walked to the canyon trail and stared upward. *Are they going to send someone after her?* he wondered. He wished they would. That way he could kill the son-of-a-bitch. But looking back to where the girl lay, he knew there were more urgent issues. *That leg's got to come off.* If she lives through that, she might make it.

Crowe watched Roman build up a daylight fire. He had covered the girl with a blanket, but she was still shivering. The marshal motioned him over.

"We're facing a dilemma, son. Kammers is within striking distance. I could be on him in less than an hour. A bullet into that jackal could end the whole affair."

"But?"

"But the girl's going to die unless that leg comes off."

Giles Roman hardened.

"Good news. If you want to call it that—no bone to saw through. That bullet already took care of that."

"I can't—"

"Yes, you can."

"Wha...what if I kill her?"

"Then she would have died anyway."

"Marshal. What yer askin..." He turned and looked at the girl. "It's too much."

Crowe grabbed him by the shirtfront. "Listen to me. This girl needs you. But those other girls, up there..." he threw a nod up the canyon, "they need me." He moved his hand from the shirt and patted the young man's cheek tenderly. "Life is hard, Giles. Hard as hell. Sometimes we have to do the hard things. If I had a choice, I'd rather stay here with you. Help you out. But this girl...this Elise. She's ain't the only one." Crowe reached behind his holster and removed his skinning knife from its sheath. He passed it to Roman, handle first.

The farm boy looked at it fearfully and then took it. It was heavy in his hand, and he hated the weight of it.

"Listen, boil up a pan of water. Put that knife in, and let it cook. In my saddlebags, you'll find a kit. Needle. Thread. I learned the hard way. A man out here needs such remedies. You'll find a flask of whisky too. Don't look at me that way. It keeps a man's belly warm cold nights. She's going to faint. Count on it. Just keep at it. She's young. Looks strong enough. But..."

Crowe had run out of words. He'd run out of strength for talking, and he was running out of time. He moved to the horses then stopped. "I'm taking your little bay. I'll leave the Ghost Horse with you. She's bigger. Stronger. That girl's pony shows a lame foreleg. If I'm not back in a couple of days, take this girl outta here. Soon as she can travel. The Ghost Horse can carry you both if it comes to that." Now he *was* out of breath. He saddled the bay then moved back to Roman and gave the young man an awkward pat on the shoulder. "Do your best, son." Then he was in the saddle and gone.

Chapter 14

Mrs. Tallit watched the odd procession—a man walking, leading a horse pulling a travois. She watched them come across the snow-dampened spring grass heading directly toward her. As they drew closer, she saw that it was the schoolteacher. The travois could only mean one thing. Something had befallen the deputy. *Perhaps he choked to death on his poor manners,* she thought and then rebuked herself. She was not a witch, and she had no power to harass a man's soul.

She glanced to see that Kip was in the corn patch with the hoe. The stalks were nothing but sprouts at this point, but he was an industrious child and liked the smell and feel of the earth. She turned back to the approaching convoy and put her hand up in a wave. Phony Landers dropped the reins and came to her, his weariness showing in his loose gait.

"You've had trouble, haven't you?" she said, looking over Landers' shoulder toward the horse and its burden.

"Ambushed. Wood's bad wounded."

Mrs. Tallit clapped her hands together as if knocking dirt from them. "Bring him inside." She called Kip from the field, and as he ran to her, she hollered that he needed to help carry the wounded deputy into the dog run's shack. It took the boy and Landers ten minutes to transport Wood from the travois to the bed in the shack where he had so recently lay. When Mrs. Tallit stared upon the lawman's ashen face, she released a moan. "Are you sure he'd even alive?"

"He's alive. Hasn't stopped bleeding, though. He's about to run outta blood, I fear. Bumpy ride didn't help."

Mrs. Tallit waited no further. Within minutes, she'd turned the little shack into a hospital, with her son as her errand boy. Landers watched her work, cleaning the wound, administering strange medicines, and finally bandaging it with clean linens. It took an hour, and when she was done, her brown hair had come loose, and strands of it fell along her temples. Sweat glistened her brow. She finally looked at Landers, who had not moved from where he'd first set foot in the room.

"I must be going," he said.

"Going? Going where? You look almost as bad off as he does."

"I need to talk to you. Alone. Outside."

The woman gave him a puzzled look but followed out into the yard. He turned to face her. "I'm asking if you can keep him here till he either dies or gets better."

"And you?"

"I'm after the man who shot him."

"Figures. You men are all alike."

"I didn't get a chance to tell you the last time we were here. We're on the trail of a band of men. They took some women. Kidnapped them."

She looked hard at him, her eyes wide. The work of a farm widow was hard, but it had not stolen everything from her. Mrs. Tallit was still a striking figure in the middle of this harsh land. "What is a schoolteacher doing chasing outlaws, for heaven sake?"

"Wish I had an answer to give you, Mrs. Tallit. But I haven't even explained it to myself yet. Too many boyhood heroes filling my head, maybe." He tried a grin, but it failed. "About Joe Wood."

"I'll keep him. Even if it means forgiving his rude departure yesterday."

Landers took a deep breath. He hated these next words, but they had to be spoken. "I wish that was all you had to forgive him for."

Mrs. Tallit's expression sobered. "What—what do you mean?"

"Ma'am. He told me a story. It explained that very rudeness. But...it explained more too. It cleared up the messy past. But it has not spoken a word yet for the future."

"For heaven's sake, Mr. Landers. What are you talking about? You do sound like a schoolteacher. Just—"

"Please, ma'am." He could not look her in the eye. "Deputy Joe Wood. He…*he* is the man that… that killed your husband."

There, it was out. The words were like hot coals, and they burned the woman deeply. She staggered backward, her hand going to cover her mouth. The shock pulled all the color from her face, and for a moment, Phony Landers feared she might faint. Or worse, commit her own crime. He heard a pig grunt in a nearby corral, and two oblivious hens came close, pecking at the ground. Her eyes had closed now, and she wiped at them. Landers felt he was at the point of death himself—death by shame for even asking for her assistance. Suddenly, she came at him and struck him on the chest with a knotted fist.

"How could you? How could you do this to me?"

Landers allowed her to strike him again, her face awash now with hot, angry tears. A light wind blew across the yard, rattling the tree branches. Moments passed. She stood still, not moving or speaking for a long time, her hands still clenched into fists. Landers believed, for the moment anyway, that she was somewhere else. Somewhere far away, deep into a time all used up, all lost. Any words he might have to comfort her had vanished, and he stood stupidly and waited.

Finally, as if drawn up from a very deep well, her words came forth. "I hate you for this, Mr. Phony Landers. And I see now just how you acquired such a name. You *are* a phony."

Phony believed he knew what was to follow. She wanted them gone. Both of them. But her words, though not compromising, were different, altogether strange.

"Don't tell Kip." It was not a plea; it was a command. "Don't tell my son. It would only bring it all back."

Landers shook his head slowly. "I wish to tell no one, Mrs. Tallit. I hated even telling you, but…it was your right to know. I only wish I had better words to follow."

"Even if you did, I wouldn't want to hear them. Now kindly get away from me." She took a step and then stopped. "I hope only to see you one more time. And that is to collect my husband's murderer." Turning her back, she strode away, leaving him standing there in the yard.

Armed with his Henry rifle, his old war Colt on his hip, and the 38 Colt Lightning hidden under his coat, Marshal Boone Crowe began a watchful ascent up through the canyon. He made the big bend as it curved around and found himself climbing at a steeper grade. The ground turned less rocky there, and a greater number of scrub trees were making their appearance. Horse signs were everywhere.

Inwardly, he regretted leaving the young Roman with such a devastating task. Crowe knew that the boy could do it so long as he kept calm. But still, two would have been better than one. When he was wounded at the Wilderness battle, he observed the gore of field hospitals. The pile of hacked limbs piled askew on a heap, covered with black flies and a stench worse even than the battlefield. A job had been given a boy to keep the camp dogs from hauling off the severed remains while soldiers were detailed to dig a pit.

But Crowe feared for the other four women. And an escaped woman could mean a rising danger for the others. Kammers, if all he had heard about him was true, was not a rational man. General Smoot was another breed of cat altogether, though. Cunning and deadly. Whoever else was in that bunch, or how many, he did not know. He was riding blind into a situation, and though he wanted to see an end to it, he had to put his own cunning to work. There were many questions he would have liked to ask this Elise girl. But she was in no condition to answer. Roman would have his hands full just keeping her alive. And if she died, he would be grief-stricken himself. Crowe tried not to think beyond that.

The canyon widened. He tried to keep to the softer earth, away from the rocks, so as not to send a ringing alarm of his approach. He rode like this for another thirty minutes and then dismounted. He was getting nervous, half expecting to hear gunfire. Gunfire aimed at him. He put the bay off the trail as best he could, took his Henry from its scabbard, and proceeded on foot, keeping to the loosely knotted pines. The sun was a hindrance now, like a floodlight shining on a stage. Creeping forward, he could feel the cushiony floor of pine needles and smell their sweet aroma. Birds sang as if it were the first day of creation, and he momentarily thought of the one-armed preacher. Crowe tried to think of what the padre would say about this situation, a lone man against many. *Do you recall Gideon, Marshal? God sent him with three hundred men against an enemy of many thousands. Gideon confused them with trumpets and the crashing of pitchers. And many enemy swordsmen killed their own warriors.* And then the one-armed preacher would flash his benevolent smile.

A mist seemed to grow out of nowhere, and Crowe stopped, peering through the trees. It was some kind of fog that clung to a clearing with a tumble of gray rocks like an enlarged fire bed. Then directly below him he saw the ramshackle frame of a decaying pole lodge. Crowe knew the kind—a sweat lodge for warriors to enter into a vision quest. Or for the ailing to have their sicknesses purified through sweat. Either way, Crowe could see it—and see also on the ground where there had been much foot and horse traffic, their markings plain in the soft soil. *Hot springs*, he realized.

He scanned the grounds foot-by-foot with minute precision, hoping to find, through the mist, any sign of humanity, a gunman, a woman, even a horse, but there was none. The women could be in the lodge, but where were the men? And where were the horses? Creeping closer, he came to the backside of the structure and peered through the rickety slats. A dying fire revealed dim orange embers, but there were no women. Were they in the hot springs? He edged around the lodge, Henry at hip level, his eyes darting from left to right, trying to see what was not there. Empty. The whole place was empty. They were gone. Moved on.

Crowe didn't know if this was good or bad. It was easy to find the horse tracks leading from the camp, heading out of the canyon and onto the flats above. Outside of the tracks there seemed no sign that anyone had even been there. Then he saw a scattering of shell casings, as if dropped on the ground from a pistol's cylinder. Six casings. Someone had emptied his gun, and Crowe figured it was whoever shot at Elise as she was making her escape.

They were ahead of him again, and if they were really heading for the Kitty Hart mine, it was clear now that they would get there before him. And though he had never seen the old haunt, he was pretty sure it would serve as a mighty fortress against him. What puzzled him most now though was why they hadn't left a rear guard. *If they know they're being followed, why not set up an ambush?* The thought gave him a chill, and he scanned once more the fog and the tree line. Then he walked back down through the canyon to where he'd left the bay.

Once the marshal had departed, Rufus Mead shifted from where he'd been hiding behind a partly fallen pine, its flaky, decaying bark reminding him of the disease-riddled men at Andersonville. He'd been stationed here by Kammers and told to kill anybody who ventured up that trail. But Rufus Mead was going through a rebirth. He didn't know what exactly, nor did he fully understand where it might lead. But his memory, if not his teeth, were still imbedded securely inside his head, and the replaying of his life was making an unexpected visitation. All he had been before, during, and since the war, seemed clearer now that it had been whilst he was actually living it. He wondered if it was an omen of some sort. Was he finally close to death?

He had watched the marshal for the hour he had spent scanning the abandoned campsite, looking for signs. The old Yankee wondered, as he watched, what it might have been like had he served out the war as an active rifleman, instead of a prisoner in Georgia's hellhole. His wandering life afterward with Lampy Dixson would never have happened. He'd have his choppers with him yet, probably, and maybe a wife and young one. It was easy to fix blame on the past, but even now the future was unknowable.

Why he had not killed the marshal was part of that unknowable reasoning. Mostly, he was just plain weary—weary of tramping it, weary of listening to the baying insanity of madmen, and weary of being on the wrong side of everything. He wanted peace, finally. Even the end of the war had not brought him peace. It had only put him down a new road of war, one of uncertainty, of hardscrabble living, and of loneliness.

Rufus never moved the rifle from where he had perched it against the fallen tree where he hid. He knew even before the marshal showed up, creeping through the trees, that he would kill no one. Sitting there he had tried to calculate his years, the before years and the maybe years, those that stretched ahead, if such years even existed. If that pretty little Rose of Sharon gal, with her battered old medicine bag had sat him down and given him a thorough going-over; her verdict, in a sweet voice, might have been, *Rufus, you're not sick, just plum worn thin.* He smiled at the thought.

The realization that he was free now came to him in the form of a tremor. It coursed through him like fresh water to a dried-up tree. Kammers had posted him here as a punishment for not giving him his pistol, so as to shoot the beautiful girl called Yelena, who'd elbowed him to the ground. Beautiful she was, as they all were to him. Even the little child, frightful of face. Sweet as a tree peach, she was. The girl should be home playing with kittens, not here with a brood of vipers, of which he had been a spineless accomplice.

After grabbing his rifle, Rufus returned to his horse. He would go back. He would follow Kammers tracks to the old mine. There were things to be done there. Amends. He spurred on his horse, the idea of freedom riding with him. It rose to the surface of his thinking now, and he pondered it mightily.

The skinning knife was sharp, and Giles Roman studied the blade as it quivered in his shaking hand. He had pulled it from the boiling pan of water and fanned it in the air now to cool it down. Kneeling beside the girl, he arranged the limp leg in such a way that he could best cut through the flesh and muscle. Earlier, while the water came to a boil, he toweled away the blood with the wetted sleeve of a spare shirt. He would use the rest of it for bindings. The fire crackled its heat. The whisky that Crowe had left him was set in the sand beside him, and though he had never touched the stuff in his life, he was sorely tempted now. *Pour it on the knife blade,* Crowe had said. *Then pour some on the wound.* He did this now. The alcohol stung, and the girl shrieked.

The moment had arrived. Elise knew what was coming. Even in her delirium, she had understood Roman's words when he told her what he must do. She cried, but when he gave her the loose end of bridle leather to bite down on, she opened her mouth obediently and pressed her teeth into it.

Roman muttered a prayer and plunged the knife blade into tissue. There was little new blood as the gunshot itself had bled much away. He worked fast, holding his breath, fearing he may gag, or worse, faint himself. As he worked, he forced himself to believe he was working on an animal, not a handsome girl. A steer, or a sow, something that might buck or bite, but nothing with a soul as sweet as Elise Prescott's. Her simple thin dress had risen up, so he grabbed hold of her upper thigh and used it for leverage. The very touch of her soft skin put a shameful charge into him.

The knife made swift work through the leg, thin as the girl was, and so he instantly thrust the knife into the fire. The blade quickly shown a hot, feathery glow, and he pulled it out and pressed the flat end of it against the stump, cauterizing the spurting veins. It sizzled and stank, and Elise cried out through the leather strip. The leg had been numb enough as he cut through, but the red hot blade forced a scream that caused her to faint.

Again Roman forced himself to work without thinking. Resting her shortened leg upon his own thigh, he took the skin and stretched it over the stump, and then taking up Crowe's simple tack, he began stitching madly, as if a demon were on his heels. The thread was thick, and it made a sickening sound as it slid through the flap of skin, each stroke pulling the repair tighter. Conscious of her body, the thin garment, and how she was placed in such a vulnerable position, he forced himself to avert his eyes. It was all he could do to keep from swooning.

At last, he inspected his work. Tearing the remainder of his shirt into strips, he bandaged the stump tightly. The bleeding had stopped, so he felt relieved about the cauterization. He washed off the knife in the water, and for the first time, he was aware of the sweat pouring from his head and face. He was soaked. It seemed like it had taken a lifetime, but now, calming himself, he realized it had only been minutes, from start to finish.

Roman lifted the severed leg and momentarily became mesmerized by it, the leg that was no longer her leg. No longer part of her body. The sole of her foot showed the cuts and marks of gravel and thorns. He felt the fool as he touched the toes and realized they were foreign now, castoffs from the rest of her. Giles had held few babies, but he cradled this lifeless appendage as if it were one. He stood finally and carried it to a place where it was out of sight. He would bury it later. Returning to where the girl lay, he took up the canteen, and after pouring a palm full of water, he drizzled it on her face. She sputtered into wakefulness.

He bent to her ear and whispered. "It's done. You need to rest. I'll watch for a fever."

She moaned then whimpered softly. Her shaking had started up again, a violent trembling that scared Roman. He touched her forehead—it was not hot, only clammy. Touching her damp hair, he stroked it, moving it off of her face. Her shaking was from cold and shock. Standing, Giles removed his gun belt and laid it nearby. Then off came his boots and his shirt. The girl needed body heat. She needed *his* body heat. Blankets were not enough. Getting down to a near naked state himself, he lay down next to her. He pulled the lone blanket over them both, and then moving close, he wrapped his body around her. He held her tight, and after a time, her trembling stopped, and her sleep became an exhausted but steady purring.

Chapter 15

As in Roman history, all roads now led to the Kitty Hart mine, though only Phony Landers viewed it as possessing such romantic imagery. And of all those in pursuit of that abandoned dominion, Landers was the only one who had actually seen it. His roaming had taken him there once, purely by accident, while serving the farm children in a schoolhouse near Decker, a small agrarian community of hardscrabble farmers and sheepherders. He had discovered it on a Sunday when he felt the urge to escape the confines of the clapboard schoolhouse, away from globes and texts and the creaking floorboards.

He did not stay long at the Kitty Hart, for it possessed an eeriness that wrangled his nerves. The town that had once been was scattered across barren, almost ugly hills where only jackrabbits and snakes might feel at home. The very ore excavating structures stood pale and silent as the fossils of dinosaurs, with multiple networks of rusting, half-uprooted rail lines coiling from the high hills into the town below.

Landers remembered that the three most prominent buildings were just as odious in their ghostliness. Both were two-storied. One, upon investigation, he deemed had been a general store and the other a saloon with hotel topside. The hotel had a balcony protruding from the second floor like a misshapen tooth. The third structure, set apart on the slope leading to the mines, was a steepled church. In and around these buildings were simple log structures, covered with moss and weeds growing through the collapsing roofs. Beyond the ugly, dry hills were trees, an abundance of them, of every variety, adding but little cheer.

And yet, here he was again, riding into a destiny as vast and unknown—and likely as deadly—as what the explorer Columbus once had. He questioned his own sanity for having come this far. He was a schoolteacher by reputation, not a hunter of killers. But something in Joe Wood had changed him—seeing him bushwhacked and near-dying; hearing his confession about the killing of an innocent man; and hearing repeated vows of hatred for the man, Othello Hardy—it put a peculiar iron in him.

Add to all of that, the women. The girls. If gallantry was a curse, then he was among the most accursed. Too many stories by Walter Scott and Fenimore Cooper. If revenge was an ill tonic, certainly justice was not. And in his most rare moment of sane-ness after being shot, Wood had thrust upon him the promise to find Kammers. And even as Mrs. Tallit was banishing him, Phony had taken up Wood's gun belt with its Colt, fastened it around his waist, and rammed the Sharps into its scabbard. His own pistol he put away in the saddlebags. He even wore the badge pushed on him by Wood.

It had all the makings of a dime novel. Only cowardice could stop him now.

BOONE CROWE LEFT THE last of the canyon country and gradu-ally found himself staring across a landscape wide and worri-some. It was *too* wide open. Far ahead he could see where the terrain angled upward again, into barren hills once peopled by fortune-seekers. Lost mines in Wyoming were plentiful, but Peach Dundee's speculation that Kammers might be headed to the Kitty Hart mine meant little. It was a place as unknown to Crowe as the pyramids of Egypt. Yet there was the trail, the tracks of nearly a dozen riders.

Riding straight there—if truly it was up there somewhere—Crowe did not fancy venturing out like a sitting duck across this ten-mile stretch of openness. A one-man cavalry charge was out of the question. He had no army behind him. No, he knew, this would take stealth. It was too late to cut them off. Best to let them settle in now. If there were no women involved, he'd go straight at them, like he had so many times before. But there were wom-en. And that made all the difference.

He nudged the bay off the trampled trail, and after a few minutes, he found a break in the plain where water from years before had cut a notch in the earth, and he rode down into it. He dismounted and let the horse graze freely on the fresh spring sprouts of grass. He needed to hold council with himself. Drawing a cigar from his vest pocket, he lit it and proceeded to wear a path in the brown soil with his pacing.

Because of what happened to Joe Wood, Phony Landers grew edgy when he saw a rider break the distant hill and head in his direction. The strange rider, leading a drag horse, also appeared suddenly apprehensive, and he pulled up both horses. The two men stared at each other across the quarter-mile distance. Neither moved for a long time. Finally, pulling Joe Wood's long Colt from its holster and resting it across the pummel of the saddle, he slowly moved toward the stranger. Had he remembered Joe Wood's telescope tucked in the saddlebag, he might have spared himself the trouble.

Likewise, the man with the drag horse edged closer. There would be a meeting in the middle, and both men were prepared for the worst. At fifty yards, they both stopped, and Phony Landers hollered out. "State your business."

"Who are you?" came the answer.

"I'm a deputy marshal." He opened his coat.

Even from a distance, the glint of the star was plain. "My name is Marcus Wales," he said. "I am looking for Marshal Boone Crowe."

Joe Wood had mentioned Boone Crowe. "What's your business with the marshal?"

The interview was growing tedious. Wales moved closer. "I was part of Marshal Crowe's posse. We were trying to save some kidnapped girls. We...well, we got ourselves separated in the storm."

Phony Landers seemed reassured enough to move up to the younger man. They sized each other up. "Kammers," he said.

Wales nodded. "That's him. You seen him?"

"No," Phony said. "But I'm expecting to."

"He's a killer, mister. Eer, deputy," Wales said, still bearing his youthful respectfulness.

"I've seen it. One of his men put a bullet through my partner."

Wales nodded. "We lost one too."

The two men, looking at each other, saw the reflected pictures of themselves—unshaven; dirt- and blood-stained clothes; heavy, sleepless eyes. They shook hands.

The long neglected road into the deserted town of Kitty Hart was a dusty, weed-infested passage into a world of ghosts and sand. The scattered buildings leaned windward, their glassless windows staring ghoulishly at the parade of riders as they plodded warily into the labyrinth of past failings. Here the wind blew ceaselessly, and even now it greeted its visitors with a witch-like shrieking as it whistled through fallen shutters and unhinged doorways.

The women drew appalling breaths at the sight of it, their eyes holding to every hint of its dark evidence of vanished prosperity. They had ruptured time, punched a very hole in it, and now their horses were carrying them into their own chapter of it. They may as well be ghosts themselves for all the hope they could expect to find in a place such as this. And there stood Mr. Smoot, his boot resting on a failing porch in front of what must have once been the hotel. He stood like a cruel specter, a welcome committee of one, straight from hell.

Kammers too, having shaken off his tremors over losing Elise, turned his horse in circles as if advertising the main event. "Home, sweet home," he said, a grin emerging across his freshly shaved face. He had taken great pains at the hot springs to make himself more gentlemanly. He tipped his hat to the women.

The girls sat mute, a mix of fear and disgust.

"We'll allow you a few days to freshen up. It has been a troublesome journey. But then," Kammers giggled, "who said paradise would come easy?" He was carrying on now like the mad actor he was. The insanity of John Wilkes Booth had been made known to the world by his actions, and here, as demented as they come, was the incarnate of the devil himself.

"But first, we must assign housing." He turned to Frank King. "Since I have already betrothed lovely Cora to you, Mr. King, I will give you the bridal suite." He pointed to the upstairs balcony.

There was a rustling of protest from Rose and Yelena, but no words came from Cora herself. She seemed, at least, to have lost her pluck at the harsh hand of Kammers at the pool, and so she sat as if frozen.

"Now, ladies, enough. We have eternity to settle just who will wed whom. Perhaps we will just become one happy commune. Share and share alike."

Rose spat, and her spittle struck Kammers on the cheek. "You are a filthy pig," she hissed.

Kammers wiped his face. "You will pay for that. You will all pay. Do you hear?" He turned his horse and faced them, his cheeks coloring violently. "Each of you will pay... for the sins of..." He suddenly stammered. "Of...for...the sins of...*Swan*." A calmness came to his voice then, unexpected, and his face contorted, as if in deep sorrow. "*She*...looked like the innocent flower, but be the serpent under't." Again, he found solace in his Macbeth.

Mr. Smoot intervened, as seemed to be his role. "Erastus," he said, soothingly, "I believe the women are weary. I believe they would like to dismount and find some peace from the trail."

Kammers, staring into a world unknown, simply nodded his head.

Rufus Mead made his way into Kitty Hart and reported directly to Mr. Smoot, who was walking the dusty lane like a town constable.

"Anything?"

Rufus grinned his gums. "Not even a bunny rabbit. I seen cemeteries more lively."

"No posse?"

"No posse. Nothin."

"All right. I've got them womenfolk putting the flames to an elk rump. Beans too. I already ate." He tilted his head in the direction of the old hotel.

"Don't mind if a do. My gums is hard as hickory. Elk steak don't stand a chance." He laughed stupidly. Then taking his horse to one of the spare shacks, he pulled the saddle and removed the bridle, patting the animal on the upper jaw. He searched his saddlebags for a small morsel of oats and hand-fed it to the horse.

Returning to his saddlebag, he retrieved a Colt Peacemaker and spun the cylinder. He already knew it held three .45 cartridges. He had silently bequeathed it to himself from the estate of the deceased Chauncey Simmons. He admired it for another minute and then stuffed it into the back of his pants inside the waistband. He concealed it with his shirttail and then tried to walk without looking like he had a burr in his britches.

The aroma of cooked meat wafted through the air as if all were well with the world; as if the happy family was having a picnic. But entering the otherwise musty hotel lobby, it was plain to see that peace and joy were not on the menu. Rose of Sharon and Yelena were sweating over the bean pot; a reckless fire smoking in the grate added to the dismal scene. The girl Cora leaned subdued against a far wall, and Hazel, curled into a ball, slept on the unkempt floor.

Toss Griffin stood nursing a plate of beans and meat, his eyes on Cora. Frank King and Erastus Kammers, sat wordlessly on opposite ends of a hewn log bench, King toying with the seam of his pants and Kammers sucking his teeth. Rufus took a tin bowl from Yelena and moved to the side to spoon the grub into his collapsed mouth. As he ate, he let his eyes move from one woman to the other. The whole room reeked of age, cobwebs hanging from every corner, the very boards moaning their discomfort at having been awakened. The absence of lamps gave the room the shadowy meanness of a tomb.

Abruptly, Kammers stood. Stepping to Cora, he took her chin and lifted it, her eyes remaining downcast. "Sure hated to break your spirit, little bird. I think I liked you better when you had some fight in you. Perhaps Mr. King would consider selling you back to me." He laughed softly. "I've ridden a few broke colts that still managed to show some spirit. I'll keep an eye on you."

King, who had been listening, spoke up. "Name your price, Kammers. I'm in a bargaining mood."

Kammers turned, smiling devilishly. "Well, since you got her for next to nothing, I'd say she oughta run pretty cheap. I doubt she's damaged merchandise. Not yet anyway. What're you thinking?"

"How 'bout a trade?" King remained seated, busying himself with rolling a cigarette. He looked up finally and stared at Rose of Sharon. Her return look was filled with venom. "If I do trade with you, Kammers, do I keep the bridal suite?"

The conversation had turned to sport, and the women were sickened by it. Rufus listened to the exchange without comment, without detectible emotion. He stepped deeper into the shadows, hoping to become invisible. Watching Toss it was obvious he was not enjoying this banter. It was no revelation to Rufus that the young cowboy still wanted to put a lasso on the sassy Cora. But the old Yankee knew what none of the others knew—a United States territorial marshal was only a heartbeat away. *So I best get to it*, he thought.

Rufus ate slow, waiting. Finally, Kammers looked at Toss as

if noticing him for the first time. "Pack it up, son. Go see if Mr. Smoot has a need for you." The cowboy clouded, tossed his plate onto a dusty table, and sulking, walked out into the street to find the old general.

"Rufus." Kammers had finally spotted him too.

"Yessir."

"Did you report to Mr. Smoot?"

Rufus made a dramatic bow. "I surely did."

"And?"

"Coast is clear. Only thing stirrin down there was some ghosts a dead Injuns."

Kammers stared at him, but Rufus meet his glare firmly. The Yankee was free now, and his freedom was like coals warming his insides. He felt bold. Rose of Sharon and Yelena remained behind the bar that housed the bean pot and the salver of elk roast. It was Rose he wished to speak to, but he dismissed it. His eyes moved across the room and fell on Cora. Moving to the bar he asked politely for a second helping, which he received.

King crossed his legs and rested his hands on his knees. Kammers considered him. "Thinking, are you?"

"Seems so. There's a heap to think about. You see, I'm a curious man. Always have been. So I see what's before us. All this. What I don't see is what's in your head. If you got plans beyond getting here, I'd sure like to know what they are." Frank King was playing his opening hand now, and Kammers' hackles were up.

Rufus decided to use this banter to move close to Cora. He had achieved his invisibility again. As Rufus moved in front of her, he let his boot lightly tap Cora's boot. When she looked up at him, he gave her an obvious wink. She returned a confused look. He immediately turned his back to her and stood there, eating his beans. After a few moments, he reached back and tugged at his shirttail, revealing the Peacemaker. He waited. Finally, he felt it being slipped from its hiding place. When he turned back to face her, he saw she had hidden the pistol under her sheepskin vest, her expression a mix of obliged astonishment.

It was impossible to whisper with a mouth void of teeth. It would come out like the unfurling of a ship's sails. So he waited until Kammers gave King a spirited reply. Then he spoke to her. "You'll know when," he said. And then he moved away. He had done what he came for—to give the girls a fighting chance. It might be their deaths, but it might also be their salvation.

Chapter 16

WEARINESS FINALLY CAUGH UP to Boone Crowe. He had already resigned himself to waiting until sunset before venturing across the open land toward Kitty Hart. Nestled in the narrow break, the bay chomping at fresh grass, he tipped his hat over his eyes and settled down for some much needed sleep. He hoped that while he slept, a clear plan might formulate in his mind about how to kill or capture four or five outlaws without harming the women. Or himself.

The afternoon sun drifted westward. He woke occasionally, listening to meadowlarks or the scurrying of quail through the grass, but he always returned to a dreamless rest. It was the sound of hoofbeats that woke him the final time, and he stiffened at the sound. His Henry lay next to him, and he had it in his hands in an instant. He braced himself against the far bank and peered over the top. The silhouette of two riders pressed against the twilight—he had slept a long time. He drew a bead on the front rider but held up, shaking his head. Refocusing, he stared over the top of the rifle's barrel at the familiar figure of Marcus Wales.

"Stop there, Wales," he hollered.

The horses shied at the unexpected sound of Crowe's gruff voice. The marshal raised his head farther, showing the Henry.

"That you, Marshal?"

"It's me. What in hell are you doing here? And who's that fella with you?"

"I'm Phony Landers, Marshal. I was riding with Joe Wood."

Crowe had not moved. "Where's Wood?"

"If he's alive, he's lying in a bed. Got shot up. Bushwhacked."

"Dead?"

"Not when I left him. But he might be now. I left him at a farmhouse." He gave no more details.

"Who was the shooter?"

"Couldn't say. He was a ways off. When I shot back with

Wood's Sharps, he hightailed it."

Crowe climbed out of the break and stood before their horses. "How'd you find me?"

"Find you?" Wales laughed. "You found us. If you hadn't popped up out of the ground, we'd still be riding."

"We caught up to the horse tracks a ways back," Landers said. "They're heading straight to Kitty Hart."

"You know the place?"

"I've been."

Crowe allowed a rare laugh of his own. He was thinking about the one-armed preacher again. *Divine deliverance,* the padre would say. "Landers, you are manna from heaven." He looked at the farm boy then and at the duel pistols at his hips. He recognized them as being Wilcox's mismatched Colts. "Wales, you got a lot of explaining to do."

Landers was off his horse now, and Wales followed suit. "You got a plan, Marshal?" Phony asked.

Boone Crowe motioned down into the break. "Gather round, boys. It's time to have a powwow."

The fire was dead. Giles Roman woke in the middle of the night, stricken with the sudden fear that Elise might be dead. At some time, the girl had turned toward him and now, relieved, he could feel her breath on his face. The demons that had haunted his sleep were chased away now with a brush of his hand. He tried to see the girl in the dark but saw only an outline. In all his life he had never been this close to a woman. But that did not mean he hadn't wished it.

He eased himself from under the blanket and dressed and then built a new fire. The danger of Kammers' hunting for them seemed to have passed. Crowe had not returned, and he remembered the marshal's parting instructions. *If I'm not back in two days, get the girl out of here.* But where to? He tried to picture a future for

Elise, who by frontier definition was now a cripple. Life was hard enough for women in the west. But these thoughts were too deep for this moment, and he shook them off.

Roman sat with his back braced against a tree and watched the girl sleep. Every once in a while, she would toss restlessly before settling down again. His mind traveled backward, to his older brothers and to the farm that would one day fall to them, being in line by birthright far ahead of him. So would the toil of it. Following behind a plow had never been to his liking. The flame in his soul was too secret to ever speak out loud, sparing himself the ridicule of his brothers. But it seemed to flare anew now, in this quiet cove, so far from home.

He allowed his mind to ponder this for a while, fantastic pictures of strange worlds far removed from the only one he'd ever known—the stark, unchanging desert of Utah. He jumped when he heard the girl cry out. Coming to her side, he saw that she was conscious. Her pinched, painful eyes stared into his, and through her ache, she murmured a word of recognition. "Giles?"

The sound of her voice, even in its agony, was a thing of sweetness to Roman. In her wakefulness, the pain had reached her again, and after freeing her arms from the blanket, she groped for his hand. Finding it she squeezed hard. Tears tumbled down her cheeks, and Roman, swallowing back his uncertainty, brushed them aside. Touching her skin was like stroking velvet, and he suddenly felt a stab of something in his chest, a pain so inexplicably joyous he could only long for more of it.

Recklessly, he bent and kissed her forehead.

Elise's tears came harder, and she covered her contorted face with a hand. She wept freely now, and Roman could only kneel next to her and press her hand. Finally, he lay down next to her again. Holding her close, he soothed her with the same gentle words he had used so many times to calm a fidgety horse. But the difference between horse and girl were worlds apart, he knew now. Touching her face again, he felt a drag on his heart, a tug, as if a cord were tied between the two of them, and with each beat of her heart, he felt the cord tightening. She was beautiful—she always had been—and he could feel his own tears coming, hidden only by the darkness.

Cora did not show the pistol to anyone. Not even to Rose. Lying in the dark, away from the others, she felt it beneath her vest, the strength of its weight, the brush of its cold metal, the grip, almost too big for her small hand. Rufus' words, *You'll know when*, had not made sense to her at the time. In fact, none of it had made any sense. Why was the crazy old man giving her a pistol? And it was loaded; she had checked. Three bullets. Maybe he wasn't crazy after all. She remembered him standing against Kammers, back at the hot springs and wondering even then if something deeper was brewing in the toothless old soldier's mind.

She listened to her own patchy breathing. Kammers had separated them, each being lead off to different buildings. Kammers had held his mock auction in the street, standing each of the women up on the trading block. The madman bragged about his childhood, about how his father had taken him to slave auctions, and about how his father always returned with a half dozen new black faces—strong, broad-shouldered men or handsome, frightened young women. King and Griffin found the thing great sport, while Mr. Smoot, as always, remained a sphinx, never taking off his mask. Rufus was not present for this sideshow, but his absence didn't appear to raise alarm.

Cora had heard Rufus' answer to Kammers' question, about whether anyone was following them. He'd said, *No*, there was no one. Now she wondered. It was Zebadiah, surely. If Rufus were bold enough to give her a pistol, then he must know something; something he didn't want Kammers to know. She now considered that Rufus might be a true ally. But when to use the pistol, and on whom, was the problem before her. Could she actually shoot somebody? She shuddered at the thought, recalling the sight of Chauncey lying on the ground before her, his very head a split gourd, sightless eyes turned upward as if examining his own ugly death.

The smell of ghosts and mildew reached her, and she covered her face with the thin blanket. A tangle of starlight crept through the broken windows, her mind at war between courage and submission.

Mrs. Tallit waited until she could hear Kip's steady breathing up in the loft before she left the house and skulked to the dog run. She carried a lamp with her, and after opening the door of the shed quietly, she moved across the floor until the lamp's glow fell on Joe Wood's face. He was asleep, his haggardness reflecting a twisting of pain. He had fought her at first, not violently, only with piercing pleas to be let alone to die. He cursed Phony Landers for bringing him here, his delirious spirit black with self-hatred.

She looked at him, sharing in his hatred. As soon as he was awake, she would demand the truth, the full confession of how he had killed John Tallit. He owed her that, and if he lived, she would get that account from him, even if she had to get it at gunpoint. In a court of law, he would be guilty of murder and hanged. Presently, the thought was satisfying.

Mrs. Tallit left him then, but did not return to the house, pacing instead across the yard to where the two cows and one horse were corralled. The cows were lying down, but the horse, upon seeing her, came to the rail. She petted its nose, and then blowing out the lamp, she moved off again into the darkness. She stood watching the moon. A soul gets used to being without someone after time has passed. And three years now had blunted the everyday pain of it. But this new visage, the actual physical arrival of her husband's killer, opened up the wounds again as if they had never been healed.

Her mind turned back to Phony Landers. She wished Joe Wood had been killed out there on the plains. Killed so Landers would never have had cause to come back here. Now she had demanded that he return and fetch this murderer. Landers' mission returned to her now, something about tracking killers. Killers who'd kidnapped some women. She couldn't remember all of it. At the time, she hadn't cared. But Phony Landers was a professed schoolteacher. What in heaven's name was he doing going after killers? Alone. What if he were himself killed?

She was standing near the corn patch now, the corn only short, green needles peeking through the dark soil. Kip, forever hard at work. He was twelve and labored like a man. What kind of future did he have? But neither the moon nor the stars gave answer to this question, and so she returned to the house. In her rocking chair, she settled once again into darkness, the darkness of a troubled soul.

Chapter 17

THEY HOPED FOR RAIN, but it did not come. Rain, or any kind of weather, might better have veiled their approach, but without it, they'd had to edge along the steep, dry hills of the mine itself, concealing the horses nearly a mile back. Now the eastern sky was giving off its first hint of dawn, a pink ribbon against the plains. Nevertheless they were on high ground, and from this vantage point, Kitty Hart spread out before them like a picture on a page.

Crowe had Wood's telescope pressed to his eye, making a slow, meticulous scan of each building and street. He saw a man planted near the road that entered the town, but he looked more interested in his boots than in the trail—the man was asleep. The plan that they had formulated between them in the night-long ride was simple. They would move as close as they could to the main buildings and then separate, each man with the same, single mission—find the girls and kill the outlaws.

They moved out one at a time, weaving through the brush, Crowe first. He wound down off the hill, careful not to raise the dust, until he came to the back of the mercantile. Wales was next, fanning out toward the building next door, which was the old hotel. Landers, as planned, angled toward the old mining tower where he had a full view of the store fronts and the main weed-infested street. He left the single shot Sharps with the horses and took up the repeating rifle instead, still wearing Wood's Colt. Wales, armed with Wilcox's Colts, also kept his shotgun with him. The marshal had his Henry, his war Colt, and the Lightning snug against his chest.

It was Crowe's hope that this could be done quickly. He had already instructed the others that it was a no-mercy situation. Hesitation of any kind might give the enemy one more chance to do harm to the girls. He had actually used that word, *enemy*, for he saw them as such. *Shoot to kill*, he'd said. Plain and simple.

Kammers was a known killer. The rest were guilty by association. Unfortunately, the first shot fired would alert the entire bunch, and true mayhem would follow. But nothing could be done about that.

Toss Griffin had not slept. Days before Lampy Dixson had given the cowboy a half-empty bottle of whisky, something to settle his nerves. This before they made their ill-fated charge across the meadow against the posse. The kid still had the bottle, and so he had drained it, swallow by swallow throughout the night. And it had worked. His courage was up.

He stepped out of the dogpatch hut he'd spent the night in, unsteady on his feet. He knew where Cora was. Kammers had stationed her in the hotel lobby after the auction, as the crazed outlaw had said — *to give our loins a chance to enflame.* Kammers was a lunatic, hot and cold, and Toss knew it was dangerous to question him. But Toss had won the right to claim Cora, at least for the time being. It was an auction without money, a hare-brained invention of the wild man, which suited Toss, since he was flat broke. Frank King had won Rose of Sharon, and Kammers the quiet beauty, Yelena. The child, Hazel, went to Kammers in the bargain.

The young, drunk former cowpuncher wavered in the middle of the street. Kitty Hart was quiet as a church at midnight. The gray haze of early morning was just burning off as the sun peaked in the distance. He stood, feeling a meanness building in him. He had not forgotten how the girl had humiliated him in front of the others. Nor had he forgotten the shameful laughter they had heaped on him. It was time for some payback.

Cora heard the boot heels strike the porch boards. She came out of her blanket, hands shaking. It would be Toss, come to claim his prize. The rage that had claimed her most of her life had been frightened out of her by Kammers. The terror of men's savagery was made manifest that day at the hot springs, and she had spent her time since realizing that life had its twists. She always thought she had control of her own circumstances, but now she knew better.

The door scraped open, and Toss stepped through. Cora instantly saw the change, the insecurity gone, replaced by a hungry sneer. Every step he took toward her echoed with devilish intent. She stood, backing away, glancing around for a way of escape, but he was before her, glowering his new menace. His hand came up swiftly, and he slapped her across the face. It stung, and she steadied herself for more, but it did not come. Instead, he pushed her against the wall. Pulling his pistol from its holster, he placed the barrel against her swelling cheek in the same fashion that Kammers had, copying the moment that had paralyzed her.

Cora could smell the whisky now, and it sickened her. Toss moved close, still clutching his pistol, and holding her face, he kissed her hard on the lips. Pressing himself against her, he let his hand move along her hip, upward, moving his hand to the bottom of her shirt, finally reaching the soft skin of her belly. Then he felt the strange prodding of something against his ribs, and an instant later, he was thrown backward by a pistol's roar.

He staggered stupidly, his eyes looking at the blood at his side. Realizing what had just happened to him, he raised his pistol, but was struck again—this time in the neck—and his pistol fell to the floor. Blood came like a spigot, pulsing from his throat, but still he stood, shocked into disbelief.

The girl's hatred blazed red. Holding the pistol with both hands now, she fired the last shot, backing Toss farther away, his shirtfront awash in blood. He shook his head confusedly, still not understanding that he was dead. His legs finally buckled, and he collapsed into an awkward heap. Gun smoke drifted before her, and still she stood, shaking now, not fully understanding what had just happened. Her free hand went to her reddening cheek, and then after touching her mouth where Griffin had kissed her, she spit onto the floor.

It was only now that Cora realized that not a single word had been spoken between them from the moment he came through the door till now. Nothing. Only death's voice.

From across the street, Frank King had scrambled outside his fallen-down shack when he heard the gunshots. He had grabbed Rose of Sharon by the wrist, and threatening her with his Colt, he dragged her across the street to the hotel. He remembered that it was the kid Toss who had won the rights to Cora. Had the damn fool killed her?

King shoved Rose through the hotel door ahead of him, but when he saw that it was Toss who lay dead, shot full of holes, he froze. He tried to make sense of it, but failing, he stepped into the middle of the room, his Colt now leveled at the girl. Finally, he laughed.

"What the hell," he said, laughing louder. "If that ain't the sweetest of revenges."

He turned then, waving his Colt to make sure that Rose had not fled. "Well, I reckon I get to claim you now. By default." More laughter. "There was an old Chinaman in San Francisco. Always preaching about karma. Looks like young Toss here ran full steam into karma."

A board creaked, and from the gloom of the backroom, a door opened. The silhouette of a man holding two mismatched Colts materialized out of the shadows. The guns were leveled at King. A moment of uncertainty hung in the air, and then King made an attempt to reach for Cora, but the Colts flamed, the double roar filling the room. Spinning sideways from the impact of the bullets, he saw Rose dash out the front door. He fired his pistol at her, but she was gone.

Wales, his face still shaded by his hat brim, fired again, the bullet striking King's hand, his pistol falling on the floor in pieces. Marcus Wales could now see that his first two shots had struck King twice, both times in the belly, and the pain had doubled him over. He sat down on the floor, holding his stomach.

"Where's Kammers?"

King shook his head. Kammers was supposed to be his. All these past days he had dreamed about killing the son-of-a-bitch. And then Kitty Hart would be his. Kitty Hart and all the women. The girl had taken care of Toss for him. But how? It didn't matter now. He thought about the Chinaman in San Francisco again. But it was his last thought.

Throughout this whole scene, Cora had not moved. With her back against the wall, she felt as if the whole world had been turned upside down. The hotel lobby drifted within its own chaos, a smoky dream that was just now silent of gunfire. The girl trembled. *Zebadiah*, she thought. *I knew you'd come.*

Finally, Wales turned to her, and the sight of his hardened appearance stiffened her. Drawing near, under the brim of his hat, she saw better his face, and she blinked in disbelief. It was Marcus Wales. The boy she had mocked to the point of torment. She stared at him, at his swarthy face, whiskers speckling his cheeks and chin, his dark, cruel eyes. It couldn't be.

"You all right?" he asked gruffly, almost indifferently.

Rose of Sharon bolted from the hotel, the echo of gunshots behind her. She nearly fell jumping off the lopsided porch, but after righting herself, she ran across the dusty street to the shed she had just left. All hell was breaking loose behind her, and she feared for Cora, but staying put might only have meant death for both of them. The crumbled, bloody body of Griffin had shocked her. Rounding the corner of the shack, she nearly fell again, and then suddenly, she felt someone grab her from behind.

She turned, trying to fight back against her attacker, and she found herself looking into the face of a gray-whiskered man with a droopy mustache and eyes the color of coal smoke. Falling backward she swung a little fist at him but missed, and she started to scream, but his gloved hand came and covered her mouth. They came to the ground together. Rose caught sight of the rifle in his left hand and tried to grab it, but he pulled it back.

"Stop yer damn strugglin, woman."

She tried to twist away, her legs kicking now. But then she saw the tin star on his chest, and all of the fight slid out of her. He lifted her to her feet like a toy doll and pressed her against the side of the building. He moved his hand from her mouth and patted the side of her cheek gently.

Crowe held Rose tight then, soothing her with tender words in her ear. "It's all right now. It's all right." After a while he felt her body melt into his.

"I saw you runnin—what happened in there?"

Rose looked up into the face of the grizzled old marshal. "They...he...the boy, he's...and King..."

"Slow down, girl. Take a breath."

Crowe watched her swallow and then sigh, her long brown hair covering the side of her face. "Cora. She. She killed the cowboy. But King. He was there. A man came from the back room. He was shooting. That's...that's all I saw. *I*...I don't know what happened after that."

"Wales," Crowe said. The hotel was quiet now, so either Wales had got his man or..." He did not allow himself to follow this thought. "Where are the other women?"

Rose shook her head. "I'm...not sure. They separated us last night."

Crowe peered around the corner of the shack, but he saw nothing and nobody. The woman came close to him, and he could feel her shaking. "Listen," he said. "If the cowboy's dead. And let's just say this King fella is too. Whose left? How many?"

Rose had to think. "Kammers. And...and Mr. Smoot."

"Two? Is that it?"

"No. There's Rufus too."

"Three then."

She nodded.

Crowe considered this, wondering who was going to make the next move.

From the building that had once served as the assay office, Kammers heard the shooting down in the street at the hotel. Yelena and Hazel heard it too. They watched him move back and forth across the floor like a nervous cat. He looked through the window, one jagged shard of glass still hanging on in the corner as a reminder of lost luck. He waited for someone to show themselves, King or Toss. And where the hell was Mr. Smoot? As he scanned the hotel front, a man he had never seen before stepped out briefly onto the porch and waved to someone, and then he ducked back inside.

Kammers turned to the girls, confusion in his eyes. "Someone's here. A posse. That damn lying Mead." He tramped back to the window, his gaze moving up the hill toward the mine's excavation tower. If he could get up there, it would be a fortress. He could hold off the world from up there. He looked at the girls, and Yelena could read his mind. She stepped in front of Hazel, waiting, her hand poised. The moment had come.

On a table lay Kammers gun belt, and he went to it now and strapped it to his hip. His rifle leaned against a far wall, but instead of fetching it, he moved toward Yelena. "Com'on. We're getting outta here." His hand reached for her, fingers gripping her shirt, but she suddenly bent over, and he lost his hold. Her hand went into her boot, and in a surprise thrust, she plunged the garden knife into his side, lodging it between two ribs.

Stunned, Kammers shrieked and fell back, holding his side, the knife still protruding, the four-inch blade buried to its hilt.

Blood came through his shirt, and he howled in rage and pain. He stumbled to her and slapped her hard. Then he grabbed hold of Hazel by the arm and yanked her forward. Yelena clawed at him, but he pushed her to the floor.

Hazel cried out, but she had no defense against him. He dragged her to the back door, and after pulling his pistol out of the holster, he kicked the door open with his boot. It flew off of its hinges, and the two disappeared, Hazel screaming and Kammers, knife still buried in his side, pulling her along.

Yelena rose, wobbly from the blow. The rifle still leaned against the wall. In his panic, Kammers had forgotten it. She went to it, picked it up, and edged around the open door. They were already fifty yards away, moving up the hill toward the mine's pylon. She put the rifle to her shoulder and tried to put a bead on Kammers, but she moved it back down again. There was no way to shoot. Not without hitting Hazel. All she could do now was watch.

As they moved, Kammers slapped the girl into silence. She fell once, scraping her knees on the rough ground, but he yanked her back up and kept going. Up the rocky hillside they went, the girl's bare feet tortured on the sharp, jagged brush. A rickety rail platform extended out from the main tower where the ore was rolled out in carts to be dumped into other carts below. It was a spider's web of scaffolding, beams, and cross beams netting below the rails. He clambered onto the planks, brandishing the girl.

Kammers stood and looked back down the hill into the streets to see if he had been detected. Nobody. But when he turned back, he saw a man standing in a dark entryway of the tower, rifle aimed directly at him. He pulled the girl in front of him, putting the pistol to her head.

"Give it up."

"Like hell."

Phony Landers did not move. He had watched them from the moment they left the assay office, hoping to get a shot, but like Yelena, he dared not. Instead, he decided to risk a distraction.

"Where's Othello Hardy?"

The outlaw jerked, as if shot. His eyes, already those of a cornered animal, darted back and forth, growing dark and distant. "Not him," he said.

"Where is he?" Landers tried again.

Kammers' face reddened, but he did not answer. His body moved with short, stiff, machine-like actions, upward, toward the rail platform, keeping Hazel between himself and Landers. Phony waited, his rifle following their movements. He watched as Kammers' head moved oddly from side to side, as if shaking off the claws of dread. He and the girl fell together on the duckboards but regained themselves.

When Kammers turned, his face was vacant, a mask of the crazed. "How dare you challenge the king! I am Macbeth."

It was Landers' turn to show alarm. A long moment passed. The schoolteacher remained fixed, rapidly racking his brain for long ago lost words. Finally, he said, "The devil himself could not pronounce a title more hateful to mine ear."

Kammers lifted a crazed smile, then followed the cue, joyous in his surprise. "No, nor more fearful."

Landers sucked in a breath. "Thou liest, abhorred tyrant. With my sword I'll prove the lie thou speak'st."

"Thou wast born of woman. But swords I smile at, weapons laugh to scorn, brandished by man that's of a woman born." Kammers stepped backward, as if to draw an imaginary sword, and for a brief second, he forgot about Hazel and loosened his grip. She sprang away, and Landers' rifle thundered. The slug struck the madman in the center of his chest, and he fell backward, his pistol tumbling through the rotting rail slats and onto the earth below.

Hazel looked up, and Landers motioned for her to get inside the tower. Something in his voice, in his gentle command, told her to obey, and she did, her tears pouring freely now.

Landers, rifle still aimed at the dying Kammers, knelt beside him. "Your charm has failed you, Macbeth."

Blood was coming from his mouth now, a trickle of it spilling down his chin and onto his throat. He looked at Landers as if looking into the eyes of a friend. *"You*… have…saved me." They were his last words, the words of a tormented soul.

Chapter 18

NEARLY EVERYONE CAUGHT UP in the drama of Kitty Hart witnessed the killing of Erastus Kammers up on the hill. It was Crowe's hope to get all the girls together and have them protected by either Wales or Landers, but at the present, it was still too risky to show their faces. Smoot was out there somewhere, and like the crafty fox he was, Crowe wondered if he might have to go house to house in order to flush out the old Confederate. Waiting was not one of the marshal's greater virtues.

The dusty streets had grown unnervingly quiet. Only tumbleweeds, stirred by the wind, broke up the stillness of the ghost town. Above, a circle of ravens blackened the sky, their dark wings making them appear dressed for a funeral.

Across the street in the hotel, Cora talked to Marcus Wales' back. He was near a window, keeping a hawk's eye on the goings-on outside. After realizing she was okay, aside from her swelling cheek, he had ignored her. The two outlaws lay where they died, the morbidity of it a sight to be avoided.

"Who all is out there?"

Wales wished she would be quiet. "Men you wouldn't know."

"I know you."

He turned on her. "No. You don't. You don't know anything about me."

This silenced her.

He could see the marshal across the street, pressed against the side of a building. They had been communicating with hand signals, mostly just to say, *Stay calm and stay put*. Finally, Cora moved up beside him.

"You need to get away from the window," he reprimanded, and surprisingly she obeyed. But she did not go far. She sat on the floor and watched him, studied him, her eyes blinking back a measure of disbelief. But she had the good sense to keep silent. Cora realized that no words she had ever spoken to him had been

151

kind, and he obviously wasn't interested in anything she had to say now.

Wales moved back from the window. "Get up," he ordered. "I'm sick of looking at these dead bodies." He headed for the stairway, testing its strength a step at a time. Cora followed. When they arrived on the second floor, they found the doors to every room hanging open, each littered with old bedframes, soiled mattresses, and fallen plaster from the ceiling. An occasional rat scurried across the floor. At the end of the hall was the entrance to the balcony, and Wales stationed himself there. Cora watched his every move, the command of his actions, the piercing flint in his eyes, and she found it hard to look away.

"Is Zebadiah out there?" she finally asked.

Wales was only half-listening. "Who?"

"Zebadiah Wilcox."

He looked away from the window and stared at her. "Not likely," he said, almost cruelly. "I buried Wilcox near a week ago."

This news was more shocking to Cora than the blow Toss had given to her face. She staggered, nearly falling. "No," she whimpered.

Wales saw the confused torture this news gave her, but he did not, at the moment, care much. It was reality, and since that showdown in the meadow, and in the storm that followed, reality was a thing renewed to him. He saw the girl's face, pale as a sheet now, the beginning of long-imagined fantasies unraveling like dust in the wind.

Up the street Yelena found herself caught between prayer and senseless murmuring. Was it really almost over? She kept a vigil at the doorway, looking up at the mine, hoping again to see Hazel, but both the child and her strange rescuer were hidden from view. The minutes dragged on.

Alongside the shack, Rose of Sharon considered her own rescuer. He was nearly the most haggard sort of knight errant she could imagine. Dust of the trail clung to his clothes like skin, his boots were scuffed, and his wide hat lined with a band of dirty sweat. He needed a shave, and his dark, stormy eyes shone like penetrating fire. His hands, free of his gloves now, were knotted with scars, and he seemed to favor one side, as if protecting a past hurt. Because she was a woman, Rose knew that that hurt could be physical, or it could be of sorrow. She blinked, her face a mild flush—here stood the most truly handsome specimen she had ever laid eyes on.

Suddenly, through the fallen roof of the little church, a cloud of pigeons burst skyward, the snapping of their wings breaking the silence. Crowe saw the frenzied birds as they took flight, and he knew that someone had just entered the building. The church's roofline had long ago lost the majority of its shingles, showing only the open rafters. The bell tower, though leaning, was still intact.

The church was set back from the main street, on a level portion of a hill where sagebrush clustered the ground all the way up to the steps leading inside. Crowe saw a shadow cross in front of one of the barren windows, and then the unexpected swish of a horse's tail; a horse concealed on the far side of the building. Whoever this was, Smoot or the other fellow, he was planning a getaway. *But what are they doing in the church?* Crowe looked at the woman and then back to the church.

"I need to get up there." He pointed. "You need to stay put, you hear?"

Rose watched the marshal pick up his rifle. "Do you have to?" she asked.

"What?"

"Do you have to go up there? If that's Mr. Smoot, he might—"

"Quiet," he said, cutting her off. "I need to concentrate." He glanced back to the church and then back to the woman. "Yes," he said. "And you need to be still. Here, take this rifle. Take it and sit down right here." He pointed. "You'll be out of sight. And whatever you do, if you have to shoot someone, make sure it's one of them." He said this with a toss of his head, indicating the outlaws. "Don't shoot my people," he added, and then he said, "And don't shoot me." Then, as an afterthought, he pulled the Colt Lighting from under his coat and handed that to her as well.

Rose took the pistol but shook her head at the rifle, so Crowe leaned the Henry back against the clapboards. "Just in case," he said.

He glanced up a weedy trail that wound its way to the church, but then he turned back. He remembered having brushed back her hair earlier and holding her close, but he had not really seen her. Now he looked into her face, saw the pucker of fear rising there again, saw the eyes, and her mouth. Her lips. He flustered for proper words. "Are...are you the one they call Rose of Sharon?"

She nodded, trembling, but meeting his gaze.

"Forgive me, ma'am. It's just..." He looked back at the church. "I gotta go."

Mr. Smoot kicked through the litter of fallen shingles, pigeon droppings, strewn papers and an occasional hymnal lying open in the muck. He marched straight for the small altar. The floorboards stared up at him like a row of hungry teeth. He walked across them, from right to left, listening for the sound of each, examining each moan and each squeak under his step. The old Rebel moved slow, as if walking on eggs, toe and heel. Finally, to the far left of the altar a board sang out flatly, different from the rest.

Pulling a chunk of metal from the debris, Smoot pried the board loose. True to Othello Hardy's word, the bank bag was in there, hidden in the darkness and musty earth beneath the altar. He pulled it out and banged the dirt from it. Inside were coins and paper currency innumerable. It had never been counted. Hardy had taken a bag with him and left the other bag for Kammers. But Kammers, with his stupid loose mouth, had taken him into a drunken confidence. And now, Kammers was dead, saving him the trouble of having to do it himself. All he had to do now was get on his horse and get the hell out. There were posse guns out there now, but luck had always been on his side, coming through the whole war with nary a scratch. *I'll claim that good luck now*, he thought.

Smoot was almost to the door when Crowe burst in, almost bumping into each other. There followed that frozen moment when recognition and alarm seem to crackle in the air, the split second before action. Crowe's Colt was out, but before he could fire Smoot swung the bank bag hard, striking the marshal across the side of his head. He fell sideways, his pistol clattering across the floor.

Crowe, on one knee, felt blood on his cheek. But as Smoot moved past him, the marshal grabbed the outlaw's leg and pulled him down. His fist struck out, hitting Smoot hard on the jaw, twisting his head sideways. He looked for his pistol, but Smoot came back swinging, hitting Crowe again. Rising to both knees, Crowe fell on Smoot, his fists driving into Smoot's middle. Tangled together, they fought through the mess on the floor, under and between the pews.

It was Smoot now who clawed for his holstered pistol. Crowe grabbed for Smoot's gun-wielding arm, and after twisting it backward sharply, he forced the pistol from his hand. Now Crowe's fist drove hard against Smoot's chin, his head snapping sideways. Both men sat, exhausted, staring at each other. In turns they each wiped blood from their faces. Smoot spoke through panting breaths. "*Hell, Crowe*...you're a tough son-of-a-bitch." He flashed a mocking sneer through the pain. "We're...too old for this kinda play."

Crowe pushed him away, and standing, they fought on, each looking for something to strike the other with. After a long struggle, they both stood on wobbly legs, out of breath, facing each other from ten feet. Crowe was blocking the door, his face bleeding from a cut on his upper cheek bone. Smoot showed the swelling of an eye and a trickle of blood from his nose.

Boone Crowe stared at him. "What is it...about you damn generals? All you ever want to do...is talk."

"You were at the Wilderness...weren't you?"

Crowe puffed bitterly, not answering.

"I heard of you. Major Boone Crowe. Hancock's cavalry outfit."

Crowe still did not speak.

Smoot saw his pistol now, his eyes moving to where it laid on the cluttered floor. "A. P. Hill gave you Billy Yanks hell that day." He nodded his gray head. "Hadn't been for Grant's love for slaughter, we'd a run you off."

Crowe silently watched Smoot's eyes, knowing the old general was stalling.

"Had we whipped you in the Wilderness...there wouldn't a'been a Cold Harbor. Or a Petersburg. Richmond wouldn't have burned and...and *Lee* would have been made king."

"But you didn't," Crowe finally said. He dove for the loose pistol, but Smoot, scrambling, got there too. In the scuffle, a single shot rang out, the bullet piercing the floor at their feet. They wrestled on, each fumbling and gouging for control. Then the roar of another shot and Boone Crowe fell back against a pew. He grabbed for his chest, blood already appearing through his clutching fingers.

Smoot wasted no time. Pushing past Crowe, he shoved the pistol into its holster, and made for the door. Out on the porch he paused just long enough to see Rufus Mead standing in the dusty street, a pistol gripped in both hands, outstretched in front of him. The brim of Rufus' battered hat rippled in the wind, and his fallen, toothless jaw appeared as a ghoulish sneer.

Smoot stared at the man, blinking back confusion. "What the hell you doing, Mead? *I*...I suppose you want the money."

"Back there," Rufus said, his voice soft and self-incriminating. "Back down that canyon...I found somethin better than money."

"You're crazy as a coot."

"Maybe. What I found was who I used to me. I found my own pitiful self, I did." The pistol did not move, and neither did Smoot. "I am a Union Yankee, sir. A once ago corporal in John Reynold's brigade. And now, I shall avenge that good man's death. I'm 'bout to kill me a Confederate general. I reckon after that, I can plum die and roll on up to heaven."

The old Colt boomed, and Smoot stiffened, the bullet striking him in the upper chest. Before he could fall, Mead fired again, and a neat hole appeared in Smoot's forehead. The old general's Confederate luck had finally failed him. He toppled off the church porch like a felled tree.

Rufus left the street, and stepping past the dead man, he entered the church. He found Boone Crowe, still conscious, trying to rise. The old Yankee knelt beside him. "Stay put, Marshal." He laid the pistol down beside Crowe "I did what I come to do." He stood then. "I'll fetch some help."

Outside he saw Rose of Sharon peering out from behind her hiding place. Rufus worked up a toothless howl. "Come along quick, Missy. Marshal needs yer help." Then he sat down on the porch and watched as Rose, swift and beautiful as a bird, sprinted up the dusty hill, her medicine bag in her hand, her long brown hair waving like a pennant behind her.

Elise woke with a steady pain in a leg that was no longer there. The sun filtering through the tree branches gave off an orange light. Through this glow she could see Giles Roman bent over a small fire, breaking up branches and putting them to the blaze. She knew him, but everything was so hazy she remembered little. Once the bullet struck her leg all coherence left her. She only recalled being taken from her horse. And then, the knife. Her leg was gone, that she knew. And she remembered Giles lying with her, keeping her warm. But she had been in too much shock and pain to put the pieces together.

Giles heard her stir so he stood and went to her. He placed his hand on her forehead. It was cool, and she watched him closely, wordlessly, as he tucked the blanket back under her chin.

"Do you feel like talking?" he asked.

Elise nodded. "Am…am I going to die?"

"I'm pretty sure you won't."

Tears came to her eyes, and she made a futile effort to blink them back. "Thanks to you." She blurted a sob. "*You*…should've let me die."

Giles showed annoyance. "I won't listen to that kinda talk."

"But. I only have one leg. What—"

"Hush," he said, cutting her off. "The marshal went off to rescue the others. And you and me. We're gonna to sit tight for a few days. I'm not putting you on a horse till you're stronger."

They were silent for a time. Giles went back to his fire. But by sundown, after eating a concoction of bacon and cornmeal, they had each shared their stories. The girl was shocked to hear about Zebadiah Wilcox.

"Cora always threatened to run away from the bishop. She had her eye on Zebadiah." Elise listened to her own words. "They were the dreams of a foolish girl. She had him pegged as a proper hero."

Giles listened in the darkness to her voice. Even through her pain, her voice was birdlike, sweet as the call of a meadowlark. "Wilcox didn't show much to me," the young man said. Then he added, "He died quick. Weren't much help to Cora."

As night came fully, mountain chill came with it, and through awkward expressions and wordless embarrassment, Elise and Giles decided it best to sleep side-by-side again.

Joe Wood stared at the ceiling of the dog run shack. He was getting used to the pain in his upper chest, wrapped as it was, in white sheet bandages. But the pain of his crimes still plagued him, and every time the woman came in to check on him, he felt like a cur dog. Her face was chiseled flint, and for the first few hours, he feared she might come in with a gun and kill him. And how could he blame her? All he wanted was to get out of there. But he didn't even have a horse. His animal was crow bait somewhere out in the saw grass.

He thought about Phony Landers. That crazy schoolteacher had showed sand, sure enough. *Where was he now?*

The latch on the door chased away the thought. Mrs. Tallit entered, carrying a tray with a bowl of steaming stew. She set it on the table and turned to leave.

"Stop," he said, shocked by his own voice.

Wood's single word was like a gunshot. Mrs. Tallit stiffened but did not turn around.

"Ma'am, I surely do not deserve the care you have given me. I know that. You would have been in your rights to turn me out to the wolves."

Mrs. Tallit stood statue-still, unmoved, only listening. But Wood had nothing more to say, so she left.

Chapter 19

THE BODIES OF THE widow makers were laid out side-by-side on the church porch. Marcus Wales had dragged Toss Griffin up the hill by his shirt collar and laid him next to Mr. Smoot. He did the same with Frank King, leaving a trail of black blood in the dust, his vanity erased in death. Phony Landers dropped Kammers' body alongside the others, then stared at them, their remains torn open by bullets, their faces frozen into vacant wonder, dead eyes revealing a strange mask of eerie disbelief. Toss' youthfulness seemed tortured, his body a grotesque abstract of splattered blood by the three bullet holes from Cora's pistol. Only Kammers' expression showed relief. Living with his own insanity had been his ruination, and he seemed finally to welcome death. A lot can be read into a man's last moments.

Down in the mercantile, the entire party of women and their rescuers assembled. Boone Crowe, having been carried from the church, was now relegated to a back room. He stubbornly refused to lie on his back, forcing Rose to administer to his chest wound while he sat on a plank bench, back against the wall. His face was ashen. Smoot's pistol had been fired at such close range that the slug passed clear through, but in its passing it punched a hole in his collarbone, scattering chips of bone every which way.

"Marshal Crowe. Your pigheadedness is not heroic," Rose said. "I need you to lie down, please. See this?" She held up a long, pointy scissors-like implement. "If you lie down, I can try to get some of those bone shards out."

This was not the worst pain Boone Crowe had ever experienced. Even the hot lead at the Wilderness was not as bad as the arrow that had penetrated his side just last year. This pain was more singularly attached to his foolish pride. He had let Smoot get the best of him, and it rankled him. There had been that moment, when he first entered the church, when he could have killed the man outright. Instead, he allowed himself to get both whipped and shot. *Have I slowed down that much?*

Rose stared down at him. "I cannot live with the prospect of you dying."

Her beseeching eyes were deep and dark. Finally, relenting, Crowe reached out a hand and allowed her to help him to the floor. She promptly put a folded coat beneath his head and told him to stay still. Yelena, who had been by her side from the beginning, knelt near him, prepared to calm him once Rose's long instrument began poking inside the wound.

In the front room of the mercantile, the falling sun spilled pink light through the barren windows and across the floor. Phony Landers sat close by Rufus Mead, engaged in quiet conversation. Rufus used Phony as the embodiment of a father confessor. He rattled through his gums a litany of somber concessions, beginning with the day he ran off to war, breaking his poor mother's heart. After much talk of Andersonville and the years tagging behind Lampy—Phony listening the whole time—Rufus got around to telling how he laid in ambush for the marshal by the hot springs. It was at this point he decided to kill Mr. Smoot instead. His days of disloyalty were over.

Hazel slept in a kitten's ball, covered with a blanket. She had hardly spoken a word in two days, but after Kammers was killed, and Phony Landers carried her back down the hill from the mine, she had asked him if he was a nice man. *I try to be,* he'd said. And then she hugged him around the neck.

Sitting near Hazel, Cora tried to swallow down a tempest of emotions. The news about Zebadiah Wilcox's death, heard from Marcus Wales' own lips, came as a shock. Even after all she had seen this past week, the cold reality that the apple of her eye had been killed, and so unheroically, caused a tremor in her heart. And the boy she and Wilcox together had mocked for his meekness, now stood as her rescuer, not ten feet away.

Even as she was trapped in a ridiculous marriage to Bishop Prescott, Cora's fantasies of running off with Zebadiah remained like warm coals inside her. She pinched herself now, trying to make herself hurt. She had left no room for either fortune or misfortune to be part of her dreams, only a long, flat surface of fanciful imaginings. As the room grew darker, she allowed herself a burden of quiet tears. Across the mercantile, the shadow of a pacing Marcus Wales flitted before her. *I no longer know him*, she thought. But then she realized she never had.

Near midnight, Boone Crowe stirred. The back room was dark as pitch, the moon a mere sliver. The wind was up, and he could hear it howl through the ragtag structures of Kitty Hart like the screaming of fretful ghosts. His wound was bandaged now, and he could feel how it had tightened. Riding a horse would have to wait another day or two. Now that the women were safe, there was the matter of returning them to Utah. He hoped that Roman remembered to meet him at Fort Tillman. There was a railhead there. They could put the women on the train and ship them back to Utah. Wales and Roman could escort them.

All these thoughts were fuzzy, and they pained an already throbbing head. Mercifully he found sleep again, and when he woke a second time, the soft light of dawn dressed the windows.

The woman, Rose, sat across the room, her eyes on him. When she saw that he was awake, she said, "You're quite a talker, Marshal."

He groaned.

"Don't worry. You expressed a great deal of peevishness towards a judge. And something about a ghost horse. It didn't make a lot of sense. At least, not to me."

His reply came slow. "I left my horse with Roman. My Ghost Horse."

This news brought Rose onto her knees. "Giles Roman? He was with you?"

"He's down in the canyon. Got my horse. And got that little gal that escaped."

Rose of Sharon was beside him now, her face close. "Elise. She's…she's not dead?"

Crowe winced, laying a flat palm on his wound. "She was alive last I saw her. Was leg-shot though. Bad. I left the boy to take her leg off."

The woman seemed almost to crumble, her words coming in fits. "Oh…we…*oh*. We were…we watched her ride. And…and Kammers *shot* at her. He wouldn't…let us go find her."

"I want my horse back. We…we're to rendezvous. Fort Tillman." He winced. "You'll git your girl back then."

"I'll go too then. Of course. I'll need to know."

"Tillman's got a rail line," Crowe said, fighting through a gruffness he felt deep in his insides. "Train'll take you all back. To Utah. Without a fuss."

Rose put her hands to her face, the word *Utah* muffled through her fingers. She stood then. "I need to tell the others. About Elise."

Boone Crowe watched her go.

A council was held in the back room of the mercantile. It was agreed that Marcus Wales would escort the women to Fort Tillman. The redeemed Rufus Mead would follow with the bodies of the widow makers, slung like the animals they were over the backs of their horses. The authorities in New Mexico and Utah would want to authenticate their deaths for official purposes. Phony Landers would depart for the farm of Mrs. Tallit to unburden her of the wounded deputy, Joe Wood. Boone Crowe would wait a day or two until he was saddle ready and then retrace his way back down the canyon to follow-up on the fortunes of Giles Roman and the girl Elise.

Rose of Sharon protested this last suggestion. "You need someone to go with you. What if—"

"I've been shot before," Crowe said, cutting her off, his voice unnecessarily sharp.

Yelena looked at Rose and saw that she'd been hurt. "She was only thinking of you, Marshal. You needn't be a beast." The young woman's ire was up. "If it hadn't been for Rose of Sharon, you'd just be another body laying over a horse."

Crowe's eyes were hooded, and he took the tongue lashing in silence. Yelena's words broke up the meeting, and everyone returned to the front of the mercantile. Within an hour, the separate parties were saddled and ready to depart. Marcus Wales was the only one who came back into the building to speak with Crowe. The marshal, resting in a corner, was hidden in shadow.

"I reckon you got some things to sort out," the young man said.

Boone Crowe grunted.

"I don't blame you much for wanting to be left alone. I'd prefer it myself. I got my own matters to think on."

"You going back? To Utah?"

"It's my wish, Marshal, to *never* see that place again."

Crowe twisted in his place on the floor. "I ain't much for talkin, son. But I'll say this. I misjudged you from the start." He stared at the dusty rafters. "Every man has a reckoning. You come through yours…in a mighty fine way. I'd ride with you anytime."

Wales nodded slightly. "I appreciate that, sir."

Five minutes later Boone Crowe heard the plodding of horses as they left the dry, deserted streets, leaving him alone with the ghosts of Kitty Hart.

Chapter 20

IT WAS LATE AFTERNOON when Mrs. Tallit, working in the upper hayfield, saw the rider meandering across the grassy flats, coming down from the north, leading a second horse. A sigh of relief ushered from her when she recognized the hunched, saddle-weary form as Phony Landers. She had not expected him so soon. At times, in the gloom of late-night contemplation, sitting in her rocking chair, she had not expected him at all. He would have a story to tell, but he would only tell it if she asked. And she wasn't sure how she felt about that yet. She removed her sun bonnet and watched his unhurried approach.

The schoolteacher had looked haggard the first time he had ridden into her farmyard, out of the snowstorm. And he was different still the second time, when he came with the wounded deputy. Then he had been worn down with the weight of truth he'd had to confess to her about Joe Wood and sobered by the violence of it all. Now, as she watched him draw near, Mrs. Tallit saw a different man. It was like studying a map, the few she'd ever seen, where so many roads and so many rivers and mountains finally led you to the place you were seeking. She simply could not put a word to what this change looked like, but it was there.

"Mrs. Tallit," he said as he rode up to her. He tipped his hat in respectful salutation.

"Mr. Landers," she said, returning the greeting. She plunged the shovel she was holding into the ground and looked up at him. "Step down, and I'll fetch you some water."

He obeyed wordlessly, following her down from the field and into the yard, horses in tow. Before going to the well, he stopped at the livestock trough and let the animals drink. After removing his hat, he pulled up handfuls of water and splashed his face, rubbing briskly. Then he threw water onto his hair and tried to smooth it back with his fingers. Finally, he stepped to the well where Mrs. Tallit waited with a dipper of cold water.

"Much obliged, ma'am." He drank and then wiped at his fresh whiskers with his shirtsleeve.

"Have you concluded your lawing?"

Phony nodded. "Justice prevailed."

She wished now to know more, but she said nothing. They stood in awkward silence, shy in each other's company. Finally, Phony looked around. "Where's your son Kit?"

She pointed casually westward. "My closest neighbors, the Mayweathers. They're calving. Kit often helps them at this time. They have no sons. They have no *living* sons," she corrected herself.

Landers twisted his hat in his hands. "Well, Mrs. Tallit, I've come to unburden you." He feared saying more than this. They both knew he meant Joe Wood, but Phony was reluctant to even speak the name.

"I believe he is as eager to leave as I am to have him gone, Mr. Landers."

Phony nodded. He had not forgotten her sharp words to him the last time they had stood in this very spot. "I inherited another horse. As you can see. I believe it belonged to the man who shot..." He let these pointless words die on his lips.

Instead, he searched his pocket for some folded bills and pressed them out flat in his palm. Two hundred dollars. Even as Rose of Sharon prepared to dig into the marshal's torn up chest with her hideous instrument, Boone Crowe patted the bank bag that lay next to him. *Open it,* Crowe had said through clenched jaw. *That's the bank's money,* Phony'd protested. *To hell with the bank. Take out enough to give that woman.* Phony shook his head. *She won't take it.* Boone Crowe closed his eyes, both from pain and from impatience. *Then use yer charm, dammit.*

Standing before Mrs. Tallit, he was pretty sure he possessed no amount of charm that would impress this sorrowful woman.

"I have here some money. I wish for you to take it. It is a cheap repayment for your services. I pray you don't see it as an insult. It is not meant as such." Phony spoke these words hastily, wanting to get them all out before the woman could interrupt. He held it out to her.

Mrs. Tallit only looked at the bills but did not take them. Instead, she turned and began walking toward the house. After a few steps, she looked back and motioned for him to follow.

Inside she shut the door behind them. "Please rest, Mr. Landers. I'll make some coffee."

Phony Landers stood in confused silence. He fully expected another tongue-lashing, not coffee. She had every right to run him off like a chicken-thieving dog. He put his hat back on and then instantly removed it and scratched his head, hoping to scuff away the mystery of this woman. He stood, listening to her tinker in the kitchen. He saw the books on the shelf again, and he stepped lightly toward them, still half-expecting a dagger in the back. He slipped the Thomas Hardy novel from the shelf and opened it, sniffing the pages. His own books had been left ignored in his saddlebags.

She startled him when she spoke behind him. "My husband's," she said.

Facing her, book still in his hand, he nodded. "That's what you said. Before."

"So I did." She sighed. "Coffee will be ready soon. Why don't you come and sit in the kitchen. I'd like to hear about these women you rescued. At least, I assumed they were rescued."

Phony returned the book to the shelf and followed Mrs. Tallit into the other room. He was reluctant to sit but did as he was bid. The kitchen offered a cheerfulness he had not witnessed in a long time. It was clean. The windows were decorated with flowered, though faded, curtains. The woman's pots and pans were assigned their ordered place on the cupboard counter. Looking down, he suddenly realized he was still holding the money. He laid the bills on the table.

"Do you take sugar? Or cream?"

"Mrs. Tallit," Phony's voice was uneasy, "*I*...I am not worthy of your hospitality. And quite frankly, am confused by it. I have done you a disservice. You told me as much not four days ago. And now...*coffee*?"

She seemed to have ignored him. She poured two mugs full and placed them on the table and then sat down across from him. Finally, she said, "Were they beautiful?"

"Excuse me?"

"The women. The ones you rescued. Were they beautiful?"

"That's a strange question, Mrs. Tallit. I...actually, I was more concerned with not getting killed myself than...than taking an inventory of their physical features. They had been kidnapped. And deprived. *And*...why does it matter anyway?"

She was studying him closely now. "How many were there?"

Phony's shoulders sank. He may as well follow her lead, wherever the heck it was going. "Five. Started out five anyway. One of them escaped but got shot in the bargain. According to Boone Crowe, she was found and saved. That's all I know about her."

"And the others?"

"Ma'am, I did what I've never done before. I killed a man. He was a bad man. He was going to kill a child—a little girl—so I killed him. It was not pleasant at the time. And...it isn't particularly pleasant at this moment, remembering it. It's my hope I never have to do it again."

Mrs. Tallit took a drink of coffee from her mug, and so Phony Landers did the same, hoping it would be an end to it. But it wasn't.

"What are your plans now?" she asked.

"I told you. I'm here to fetch Joe Wood. He lives down south. Wakesville. I'll return him to his ranch."

"After that?"

"Please, ma'am, you are asking me questions that even I don't have answers to."

"Of course. I'm sorry." Even as she said this her eyes did not leave his face.

Phony fidgeted uncomfortably. "I truly reckon I oughta be going. I should be checking on Joe. Making sure he's up for a ride."

"He's ready. But..."

He wanted to ask, *but what*, but feared the answer, so he said nothing.

She stood suddenly. Stepping to the counter, back to him, she stared out the window. "It has been three years, Mr. Landers."

Phony waited.

"Three years since I have heard a man's voice. At least a man's voice that wasn't old Hap Townsend over at the junction. Or Mr. Mayweather, who barely speaks to his own wife. And not your wounded deputy. They don't count. And they have never sat across the table from me with a cup of coffee between us. You are the first in three years. And so...*if*...so if I am acting like a foolish old hen, then so be it. I make no apologies."

Her voice was neither weak nor pathetic, only matter of fact, and Phony listened with interest. "I thought you hated me."

She laughed a tiny laugh. "I did. And maybe still do. It's a woman's prerogative to love or hate whoever she sees fit. And it can change. Just like the wind, Mr. Landers. Just like the wind."

It was Phony's turn to study her face. He could only see her profile as she continued to gaze out the window, but what he saw was what he had seen the last time they had spoken, when she had driven him off with her harsh words. It was a handsome face. Neither the sorrow over the death of her husband nor the hard work of raising a boy and keeping up a farm had stolen what she must have had since her youth—a strong beauty.

"Loneliness is the mother of forgiveness, Mr. Landers. Forgiving you is a mite easier than forgiving your partner out there." She turned to him now. "Everything has its degrees."

Seeing her now, Phony saw that there was dignity in her face. "Why don't you come back to the table, Mrs. Tallit? Let's finish our coffee. And I'll...well, I'll try and put an answer to your question."

She sat. Then hesitatingly she reached across the table. Phony, acting on instinct, took up her hand and squeezed it.

It was an hour later, even as twilight was spreading across the land, Joe Wood, favoring his wound, sat on his horse. His own sorrow now seemed to outweigh the widow's, but he knew any words coming from him would be empty to her ears. Phony Landers stood beside his horse, facing the woman.

"Thank you for the coffee, Mrs. Tallit. And for everything else." He nodded toward Joe Wood.

"Thank you for the conversation, Mr. Landers. Will you be back this way?"

Phony searched her eyes. "Is that an invitation?"

She gave him the only smile she'd ever allowed him. "If it sounds like one, then it must be," she said.

With night coming on, Boone Crowe did not linger. He had enough ghosts haunting him without needing the ghosts of Kitty Hart to join the party. With delicacy he saddled Giles Roman's horse. He put the stolen bank money into his saddlebag, took one last survey of a town he hoped never to see again, and rode slowly away. He made the hot springs by dark, weak and bleeding anew.

After tending to the horse, he stripped down and eased himself into the warm pool. He settled in, water to his neck and gingerly touched his wound, the gray water turning pink from the blood. He slept like that for an hour, a foggy prayer beseeching the pool's waters to lend healing. When he finally stirred, his chest felt tight, the grotesque flesh pulling together as if on the treads of a spider's web. He submerged himself fully then, scrubbing at his face and harrowing his fingers through his tangled hair. When he came up for air, he saw the moon through the trees.

Dressed, he saddled the horse again and continued down through the shadows of the canyon trail. Boone Crowe knew where his troubles lay. It wasn't the bullet that had torn through the right side of chest that plagued him. It was the wound to his heart. It was the woman. His hand went to the watch in his vest pocket, the watch with the small, dark photograph attached to the fob. It was the better likeness of Eva. The only other lingering image of her was one he wished he could erase from his memory. The picture of her in death. At Dead Woman Creek. Near Dry Branch. She was buried on the hill there, left to the care of the boy, Tanner Hornfisher. The only woman he'd ever loved.

Crowe might have ridden all the way to California had his mind been on the business of riding, but it was wavering dangerously between the bitter past and a random future, a future in word only, a universe away, as empty as a burnt-out star, falling through a dark sky. It had been wise to end it. Good to send her away with the other women, with Wales. The young man would put them on the train, and by the time he himself got to Fort Tillman, they would be gone, back to Utah. *But...* he thought. How easy it would have been to let her stay. To tend to his ailments.

The marshal might have wept now were he not so angry with himself. How life seemed to twist at his insides. He was a man of fifty, broken of body. War damaged. Haunted by a thousand deaths. Could even Eva have put his pieces back together again? He would never know. A lawman sick of lawing. Lost in a sea of want, rudderless.

The sight of the old camp, hidden in the grove of trees, brought him out of his reverie. It was plain to see that Roman and the girl were gone. A cold camp of ashes was all that remained. Dismounting, Crowe searched the grounds, thinking that if the girl had not survived she might be buried nearby. But there was no sign of a grave, and even in the moonlight, he could see there were mismatched footprints in the dirt, one with boots, the other a single bare foot.

Crowe's wound had become a steady, pulsing throb now, the bleeding stopped, a pain he could deal with. The other pain, that of a woman's face, and now, a second woman's face—that pain lingered. Without fully realizing it, he had remounted and was down through the canyon again. Roman would be traveling slow and resting a lot. He might overtake them by daybreak.

Sometime in the hours of pink dawn, while dozing in the saddle, the face of Rose of Sharon entered his half-dreams, and the warmth of it was not unlike the waters of the hot springs.

Chapter 21

THE CARAVAN MOVED SLOWLY through the day and then rested for the night. On the second day, they moved again, out of the high country and into the vastness of the Wyoming plains, with the sawgrass and sagebrush coloring the low hills. Antelope were about now, in great numbers, their gray, horn-spiked heads watching from above the meadows. Rufus Mead hung back from the group with his cargo of blanket wrapped corpses. They had begun to let off an odor, and though it was a stench that Rufus was well accustomed to from his wartime captivity, he did not want to offend the women by following too close.

As afternoon waned, they rested by a stream, and the women spread out in welcome repose. The water of the stream was clean and cold and fast-running, so they drank from it. Rufus, taking one of the captured rifles, rode over a hill, and an hour later, he returned with an antelope across his saddle. By sundown the shanks of the animal were well roasted over a fire.

During the two days of travel, Marcus Wales had spoken little. He gave an order once in a while, comprising mostly of when to stop and when to break camp. Otherwise he was all about his own business. His great transformation, as he viewed it, was still a work in progress, and in his new found wisdom, he figured it would extend well into old age, if such a thing was granted him. He kept his distance from Cora, though he was well aware of her eyes on him. Her brashness, as he remembered it—and had frequently suffered from it—seemed to him to have been replaced by a somber curiosity. He no longer felt her bitter judgment, as before, rather this curiosity, a sort of confused, unfolding wonder.

As for the rest of the women, Wales knew that a day of reckoning was near. There were questions to be asked and answers hoped for. If he didn't know their minds, he at least needed to share his own mind with them. Wyoming was a new country to him, and it was beginning to embrace him with its wild appeal. Still, he needed to be vigilant. Indians were no longer the threat they had once been. But his experience in this past week educated him toward an alertness to the unexpected. With the supper eaten and his thoughtful pacing completed, he chose this moment to face the women.

"Begging yer pardon," he began, speaking slowly and swallowing down his nervousness. "Being unfamiliar with this territory, I do not know how long it will take to reach Fort Tillman. It was Marshal Crowe's instructions that I take you there. In order to catch the train back to Utah. I told him I would. I suspect it will take a few days more."

The women listened to him, and his voice was remarkably steady.

"The marshal said to go due east and we'd find it. This we will do. However..." He paused here, looking into the faces that were staring back at him. "I advise you give these next hours... these next *days* to considering your forthcomings. If you haven't already."

The women now glanced at each other, faces searching faces.

"As for myself," he continued, "I will not be returning to Utah. I tell you this so you will know that if you go back, I will not be going with you."

This confession came as a surprise to all of the women, even the girl Hazel, who knew well enough that the Wales clan were big ranchers in the area, second only to the Prescotts themselves. A murmur rose among them.

As if this news gave them permission to express their own thoughts, Yelena spoke up. "Nor will I," she said. "I was put on the orphan train when I was too young to have a say. But I'm not a girl anymore. I feel I have been made a widow by God's hand. Surely that train goes someplace that isn't Utah. If it does, I'll go wherever it goes."

Hazel erupted into tears. She covered her face with her hands, but no words came, only sobs. Yelena told her to hush and drew the girl into her arms.

Rose of Sharon spoke next. "The marshal told us about Elise. That she was with the Roman boy. Giles. They are to meet us in Fort Tillman. At least, that is the hope. I plan to wait for her. For them."

"What about the marshal?" This from Yelena, but it was directed to Rose, not Wales.

Rose lowered her head. "He didn't say."

Marcus Wales allowed himself a hasty glance in Cora's direction, but she only sat in silence, her fingers toying with a blade of grass.

Boone Crowe knew the country. He sat on Roman's pony and surveyed the panorama in all directions. He had ridden out of the canyon country from where so many strange and deadly happenings had taken place. After another day of aching shoulder pain, he used an unlaundered shirt to secure his right arm into a sling in order to relieve the strain on his chest. Ahead lay Fort Tillman, days away yet. Far north was the Yellowstone country and farther south, in lush cattle country, lay the hamlet of Dry Branch. He looked in that direction for a long time.

The one-armed preacher would accuse him, *You've got a drag on your heart, Marshal.* Around the padre Crowe always felt he was transparent. As if he possessed neither skin nor bones, only a see-through invisibility, something that gave the preacher the ability to gaze clear through him. Into his heart. Into his mind.

Finally, he looked northeast, toward Buffalo. He had only two payments left on the little ranch he had coveted for these past six or seven years. Saved for the retirement he doubted he would ever see. Eva was gone, and it was her ghost he had always seen haunting him there. The gunshot that Smoot had punched through his chest was a reminder that he was on death's trail. It was only a matter of time.

He rode east again, but not in haste, and toward evening, with rain clouds moving across the sky, the war revisited him, the echo of its guns, the cries of horse and man. The smell of cannon smoke and gun powder. Picket duty with Seth Holland. The thoughtful pacing of General George Henry Thomas, the best general, by Crowe's reckoning, in all the Union. Then back to Virginia, to Hancock and the Wilderness. And Cold Harbor. And all the days that followed after Appomattox. The quiet days of uncertainty when the countryside fell silent of gunfire.

Crowe played it all out again as he rode.

As a light rain began to fall, the chaos of Kitty Hart came back to him. For all the miles and days of tracking that odd band of cutthroats, he realized that he had not laid eyes on any of them, save Smoot, and even that, only in the flurry of fists. The plan that he and Landers and Wales had laid out, that of dividing and conquering, had worked out well. Each entering a separate building, allowing for surprise, one-on-one confrontations proved successful. Had the outlaws been grouped in a bunch, it would have been a war, and in that kind of shootout, someone might have been killed, like Wilcox had.

It wasn't important that Crowe hadn't seen their faces. He'd killed many in the war that remained faceless. Maybe it was the time invested, and the sacrifice of Wilcox and the girl, Elise, that ate at him. He had stumbled into a man in the church that he should have killed outright, without questions. It was a clumsy, careless mistake.

Crowe spat. It was that damn pride of his, eating at him like a cancer. He knew it. He was angry because he had done nothing to help in the fight. It was supposed to be his show, as it always was. After all, he was the marshal, and it was his job to get things done. Instead, it had been a reformed farm boy and a book-smart schoolteacher who had rescued the women and killed the murderers. Even Smoot had been killed by one of his own. All he got for his trouble was to get himself beaten and then shot.

There was more too. Worse even. The woman.

In this moment of hard truth, Crowe raged in the rain. For that brief impulse, when he had held her, his arms around her, the echo of gunshots coming from the hotel, he'd been jarred by something. A thunderbolt. Then, touching her hair where it covered her face and looking into her frightened eyes, he felt a loosening of his armor. A sudden, terrible flash of passion. He feared it showed in his face.

But then, in defeat, it was she who had saved him, the touch of her hands more painful even than the wound. And in his pride and his shame he had treated her poorly. Another log now thrown on his fire of self-blame. *I made a fool of myself,* he thought. *And thinking about her now jist adds to my foolishness.* Crowe felt like running away. The very absurdity of love to him was represented by an open grave. He thought of Mexico. *Damn pretty place in springtime.*

Folks busy on the streets of Fort Tillman stopped what they were doing and stared at the man and woman—she with only one leg—as they rode doubled-up on the big, pale horse. Elise kept her head braced against Giles Roman's back, eyes closed, oblivious to the gawking citizens. Roman's intent from the beginning was to ride straight to a doctor and have him look at the girl's stump to make sure his handiwork was worthy of healing. The young man kept his own eyes directed squarely forward. Here was a place like none other he'd ever seen. Towns in Utah—the few he'd ever entered—were tamer in appearance. This town, this Fort Tillman, seemed a mixture of wantonness and piety. There were saloons aplenty lining the streets, but there were dress shops, too, and drugstores and even a bookstore.

Roman saw the shingle hanging about the door, reading, Dr. T. T. Wills, and so he drew up to the rail. After swinging his right leg over the horse's head, he slid down from the saddle. Reaching up then he lifted Elise into his arms, carrying her like a bride upon the boardwalk. He kicked at the door and waited. A man with a white beard and dusty boots left his perch by the dry goods store and opened the door to the doctor's office.

"Much obliged," Roman said. He carried Elise inside, the man following, and he sat her down on a bench.

"Hello," Roman hollered.

After a minute, a bespectacled man appeared through a curtain and took in the scene before him. He looked from Roman to the girl and then back again. "What's this?"

"She needs looking after," Roman said. "I done the work myself. It ain't pretty, but it's held up so far."

"What happened?"

"Gun shot."

Doctor Wills pardoned himself as he bent to the girl. Taking the stump in his hands, he unwrapped the simple bandage and gave it a concentrated examination. He inspected the stitches and putting his nose close, sniffed for any signs of infection. After several minutes of this, he stood and looked at Roman. "You did this?"

The young man nodded, nervous. "Yessir."

The doctor returned the nod and rubbed his chin. "I think we'll leave it as it is. It's tolerable good work, considering. Where are you staying? She needs rest. That'll be the best thing for her. And I can check on her again later. See how she's doing."

"We just rode in. And we've scarcely a dollar between us."

The doctor noticed the bearded man for the first time. "Cassis. Go down to The Emerald and have Zeke make up some grub. Sandwiches. Have him put it on my tab."

The bearded man named Cassis left without a word.

"Now, listen up, young man. This girl needs rest." Leaving Elise sitting on the bench, Doc Wills took Roman by the elbow and led him out to the boardwalk. Pointing up the street, he said, "Out at the end of town, another quarter mile you'll find a tent town. It's a whore's haven, sure enough. But they're harmless. On one side of the dirt path you'll see a big gray tent with a cross painted on the side. Belongs to a preacher. He has a couple of tents up there. He's a good man. He'll take you in for as long as you need."

Giles Roman nodded.

"I mean it."

Roman nodded again. "We'll do it."

"See that you do. And…" He put his hand on Roman's shoulder. "After you get settled in up there, I'd like to see her in a couple of days."

They stood for a few minutes longer, taking in the crisp, fresh, morning air. "Is she your wife, son?"

"No, sir," Roman said, embarrassed.

Doc Wills nodded. "Leg or no leg, she's an awfully pretty little creature. You may have figured this out by now, though. But what you did, by cutting off that leg. You saved her life. Had you not, she'd never have made it this far. She'd be dead by now."

Through the window Roman could see her, sitting quiet as a sparrow, her hands in her lap, her brown hair ashine.

Joe Wood was not much of a talker, even in the best of times so Phony Landers endured his long silences by thinking his own thoughts. The action at Kitty Hart had already taken on the form of a surreal dream. Fueled by his own rage at seeing Joe Wood shot down—a rage he didn't know he possessed—had carried him through. But now, having already removed the gun belt he'd used in the fight, he hoped to log it away, a story meant for grandchildren someday. His one heroic act, by spouting Shakespeare, he had managed to save a young girl from the clutches of a madman. It sounded like made-up literature.

Phony was already picturing the telling of this story to a schoolhouse full of adventure-hungry pupils when Joe Wood woke from his brooding.

"Did Kammers ever mention the name of Othello Hardy?"

181

"Afraid not," Phony said, wondering why it had taken so long for the subject to come up.

"Nothing?"

"Nope. He had plenty to say about Macbeth, though."

Wood's face darkened. He leaned forward over his horse's neck, relieving the pressure on his shot-up shoulder.

"I met a fellow, though. Name of Rufus Mead. Ever heard of him?"

"No," Wood said, testily.

"He rode with that bunch of cutthroats. But in the end, he killed Smoot."

"That's nice. A regular do-gooder."

"You might say that. He didn't have a tooth in his head. But he had ears."

"Meaning what?" Wood was already bored with this small talk.

"Meaning, that he overheard a conversation between Mr. Smoot and your Erastus Kammers."

Wood straightened up in his saddle, his face a grimace of pain.

"Seems Kammers, in one of his fits of madness, said something to Smoot."

"And?"

"And my man Rufus heard the whole thing."

"Dammit, Landers. Stop playing with me."

"Rufus Mead told me that he heard the name Othello Hardy mentioned in this conversation. And that Kammers planned to meet up with him. Once they had tamed the womenfolk."

"Where? Where was he gonna meet him?" Wood was alive now, bright-eyed and hanging on to Phony's every word.

"Well, he didn't exactly give an address, but—"

"Spit it out, Landers."

"Don't be so cranky. I'm getting to it. First, he said Buffalo."

"Buffalo. Hardy's been in Buffalo this whole time?"

"That's what I thought. And I said as much. But Rufus corrected me. Kammers had said...Hardy was long gone. All the way back to Buffalo. Buffalo, New York."

Phony heard the wind come out of Wood like air from a balloon.

Near dark Joe Wood's ranch came into view through the valley walls. The deputy had not spoken a word for hours. Phony reined in, and Wood did the same.

"You might as well come down. Ortega can get some grub up."

"I'll pass, Joe. I'm still a wanted man in these parts. You know. The infamous bull slayer."

Wood only nodded.

Then Phony reached in his pocket and retrieved the deputy marshal star that Wood had given him after he'd been shot. One of the star's prongs had been slightly bent from where the bullet his struck him. "Reckon I don't need this anymore," he said, handing the badge back to Wood.

Wood took it, looked at it, his thumb stroking the bent prong. He then put it in his own pocket. "What's next for you? You heading back to your cave?"

"Not sure. I might go back to teaching school. But I doubt it. I've some thinking to do on that." He thought of Mrs. Tallit. "Funny. I always seem to think better over a cup of coffee."

Joe Wood nudged his horse forward and then stopped. "I ain't much for givin thanks. But I reckon I owe you one."

Phony moved up alongside and holding out his hand, they shook. "Things happen, Joe. Might be time to forgive yourself. Even if others don't."

They shook again. "You'd make a lousy preacher, Landers." And then he rode away, into the darkness toward the dim light of his ranch house.

Chapter 22

A MILE BEFORE REACHING the main streets of Fort Tillman, Marcus Wales and his caravan passed a clapboard schoolhouse, set against a hill with a lone tree and a small house out back. There was a bell on a post with a rope hanging from it, and standing in the doorway of the school was a tall, handsome man in a dark suit and trimmed beard. The man waved, and Wales waved back and then called the women to stop.

"I'd like to get a fix on things before we just go riding into town," he said. There was a patch of short grass with two rough-hewn benches, and he indicated that they might as well get down and stretch their legs. The women were happy to oblige. Rufus Mead hung back with his ominous cargo, but Wales dismounted and walked up toward the schoolhouse.

Wales nodded a greeting, and the schoolmaster met him in the foot-beaten dirt of the playground.

The teacher, showing a welcome grin, raised an eyebrow. "I'm busting with curiosity at your little company." Both men turned and watched the women settle onto the grass, and at the horses bearing the bodies of the dead men. "Name's Axel Harrington," the schoolmaster said, putting out his hand.

Wales took it and they shook.

"Begging your pardon," Harrington said. "But you all appear a bit worn down."

"I'm Marcus Wales. And worn down is the plum truth of it."

They stood in awkward silence for a moment, watching the women, and then Wales said, "Where's your pupils?"

"It's Saturday," Harrington said, good naturedly. "It's hard enough getting them here during the week." He smiled. "Anyway, we have a well out back, Mr. Wales. Why don't you have your womenfolk freshen up some."

"I appreciate that. *And*…as you can see, I've got business in town. I'm supposed to meet the marshal here."

"The marshal?"

Wales nodded. "Boone Crowe."

Axel Harrington gave out a hoot. "Boone's coming here?"

"You know him?"

"Ha. Everybody knows Boone Crowe. Why, he was best man at my wedding. And trust me, Mr. Wales, getting him in a suit and tie was near hard as wrestling a grizzly."

Both men stood in their own revere for a moment, and then Wales gave Harrington a brief history of the past week, explaining the dead bodies and the weary state of the women. He told of Crowe getting shot and Harrington, showing no great surprise, said, "That old buzzard. He has a way of stopping bullets. And Ute arrows."

"We left him in his stubbornness."

"That's Crowe all right."

Axel Harrington's wife came from the little house then and joined her husband, taking his hand. It was easy to see that she was an Indian. Her skin was deeply tanned but soft as a lily's petal, and her dark eyes shown sunnily. Wales was struck by her handsome features but said nothing. Harrington gave introductions and then all three walked to where the women rested.

"Pun'ne, why don't you show these ladies where the well is. And then we'll get some hot food for them. No reason to go all the way into town. Folks would think they were going to a circus. Besides, there's plenty of room in the schoolhouse for a day or two. And...it's not every day Pun'ne gets the company of womenfolk."

Shortly, Marcus Wales and Rufus Mead made the last half mile to Fort Tillman with the bodies of Kammers, King, Toss, and Smoot in tow, their entry into town causing no little amount of interest. Delivered first to the sheriff and then to the undertaker, the two oddly-matched companions went back to the sheriff and spent several hours giving him the whole story. It was the sheriff who made mention of another young man, fellow by the name of Roman, and a one-legged girl, arriving just the day before, offer-

186

ing Wales directions to where he might find them.

At the schoolhouse, the widows of Bishop Prescott told their tale, Yelena doing most of the narrative. Then Axel Harrington and Pun'ne gave a telling of their own wild experiences in the desert of Nevada, culminating in a showdown at a rail water stop called Rattlesnake Wash. The one name that continued to evolve into the center of these accounts was Marshal Boone Crowe and the grit he had shown. In the homey setting around an outside fire pit, where everyone was gathered, it was Rose of Sharon alone who listened keenly but remained silent throughout.

The shock of seeing Marcus Wales was no less great to Giles Roman than Wales' shock at seeing Elise. Roman and Elise were catching some spring sunshine outside the tent chapel of the one-armed preacher when Wales and Rufus rode up. The very sight of Wales was shock enough, but seeing him with a pair of mismatched Colts—which he immediately recognized as Wilcox's—gave Roman a start. They gave each other a warm greeting, and then Marcus moved to the young woman and knelt before her.

"Everyone's safe, Elise," he said. "All the womenfolk. And…" nodding toward Roman, "and I'm pleased to see you are safe too."

None of the ordeal had taken the prettiness out of her face. "I think the doctor has his sights on Giles," she said. "Says he needs an assistant." Her speech seemed sweetened by rest and shyness. She removed the blanket from where it covered her lap, and she pointed to the stump, a peculiar kind of pride in her voice. "But Giles don't seem too interested." She made a small, birdlike laugh.

Giles, standing near, let his fingers brush Elise's hair, and Wales saw the meaning in that. After a minute, the tent flap parted and out stepped the one-armed preacher, a thin man garbed in black, a broad grin on his face. "Greetings, my friend."

Wales' eyes moved from Elise's missing leg to the preacher's missing arm, a slow awakening of coincidence, if such a thing was coincidence. After all he had been through, he was not much of a believer in chance. From his grueling night in the storm where he traveled through the grip of fear and self-hatred to what he was now, the notion of mere fluke had been washed away with the tempest.

As if reading Wales' mind, Elise said, "I came here last night as a cripple, Marcus." Her eyes went to the preacher. "But thanks to the kind reverend, he showed me that isn't so."

Roman and Wales took a short walk through the mud-lined street. Whores, hanging up their laundered petticoats and underthings on a community clothesline, watched the two young men with joyous appraisal. At one point Roman stood back and took in his friend with amazed wonder.

After a while, the two visitors rode away. Rufus gibbered a laugh.

"What's funny?"

"Love."

"That's it? Love?"

Rufus laughed again. "That's it."

Rose of Sharon made a pretense of wanting to watch the sunset from a hilltop, but what she really wanted—and needed—was some time alone with her thoughts. She had weighty matters on her mind. Yelena had made her intentions clear enough. She was going back east on the train. And the prospect of Hazel going with her seemed obvious. Yelena had been brimming with courage from her very first arrival on the orphan train all those years back. It was her sharp mind too that had kept her from the clutches of the bishop. Further, she had been little short of a mother to Hazel. They seemed to need each other.

Cora, on the other hand, remained a perplexing riddle. Or at least she had turned into one. Her once irritating brashness had been challenged in the hot springs when Kammers put the fear in her. But she momentarily regained some of it at Kitty Hart when she shot dead the young cowboy, Toss. Even that, though, was an act more of fear not courage. Fear and hatred. The stupidity of her youth, in having tortured the Wales boy, had come back to roost in her tree. He appeared to want nothing to do with her, and who could blame him? Wales himself made it clear he wasn't going back to Utah. *If Cora decides to go back,* she thought, *then I'll have to go with her.* At present, it seemed her horse Stella was the only friend Cora hadn't offended.

And what about me? Rose stood on the very threshold of uncertainty. From the time of her coming to Utah, she had given herself to nobody. Back east she would be, at thirty-five, considered an old maid. A spinster. But this wasn't the east. It was the west where men greatly outnumbered women. Her bond to Prescott had been in name only, a bond which, with a single gunshot, had made her a widow. She had never felt married. Not to Prescott. Not to anyone. There were men in Utah who would have her, but she never again wanted to be one wife among many.

Rose stared into the deepening sky where the falling sun was laying down a pink gloaming. Wyoming was a beautiful country despite the danger it had inflicted on her recent life. The mountains were still silver with snow, and the wind gave music to the tall grass. The antelope were so plentiful they seemed like playthings. It was no wonder this was the place Boone Crowe chose to live.

The sudden thought of the marshal touched her. *Of course,* she thought. *This is his country.* It was not a bitter thought necessarily. More sad than bitter. In his pain and delirium, when she was probing his wound with her knitting needle-like tong, he had uttered a name. *Eva,* he had said. He had said the name two or three times. It was all the answer she needed.

Rose felt a catch in her throat. The sun was down now, but as she turned to go, she saw the shadow of a man standing near the bottom of the hill. Startled, she took a step backward.

"It's only me, ma'am." It was the voice of Axel Harrington. "May I join you?"

"Of course. I was just enjoying the sunset."

"Had you noticed, you would have seen the ground beneath your feet trampled by my nightly visits. It's my favorite place to say good-bye to the day." He came up alongside her and stared into the darkening night.

"I've kept you away from your nightly visit," she said.

"Not at all. I have no claim on this country. Or of the sun when it goes down." He said this good-naturedly.

She gave a humorless laugh. "No. It appears Marshal Crowe has a claim on that."

"That's partly why I came up here, ma'am."

"Call me Rose. Please. But...why—"

"Hunches. I used to be a newspaper reporter. Started in St. Louis. Then Reno. Gave it up when I met Pun'ne. But newspapering is all about hunches, Rose."

Their faces were barely visible in the dimness of evening, but their voices were clear.

"You said Boone Crowe was the reason you came up here. What do you mean?"

"Pun'ne and I told you of our great adventure in the Nevada desert. And we had some fun at Boone's expense tonight. Yes, he's a gruff old badger. A gruff old badger with a heart of gold. I've seen him in all his heroic glory, Rose. And I've seen him, like you have, flat on his back, bleeding from wounds that should have killed him."

Rose shuddered but not from the chill of night.

"Are you a fighter, Rose?"

"Excuse me?"

"Begging your pardon, but I watched you tonight around the fire. I watched your silence. And the girl Yelena. I watched her watching you. Later on she told me about how you patched Boone up. I reckon a woman knows more about how a woman feels than a man does. But it was my impression, from what Yelena said, that you felt the old cuss was worth saving."

"I was only doing my duty, Mr. Harrington."

Harrington nodded in the night. "Maybe. But let me tell you something that Pun'ne and I didn't say about Boone. In fact, I don't even think my wife knows. But I know. And...following my hunches again...I think you ought to know too."

Rose of Sharon stood rigidly, arms at her side, waiting.

"Some years back Boone was planning on getting hitched. The gal was overdue on a train from Omaha. When he finally found her, she was dead. She had been murdered. He tracked her murderer and killed him. But he's been a torn-up man ever since."

"Eva?"

"Yes. Eva Gist."

"He...he spoke her name. When he was..." Her words trailed off.

Axel stepped closer. "I'm assuming a lot here, Rose. Forgive me. I may well be off my rights to even imply such things. So let me just say, Boone Crowe is an honorable man. But he is a haunted man too. Haunted by the war. And haunted by Eva. But he is my friend. And I do not wish for my friend to be haunted forever."

Rose listened. Axel Harrington's words seemed to play out in the night like a chain of stars. "Is that why you asked me if I was a fighter?"

"Boone Crowe is prime for picking, Rose. If you get my meaning. The only one who doesn't know that is Boone himself. Give him time. He might figure it out. If he doesn't get himself killed in the process."

They stood in silence for a while longer, each studying the sky. Finally, Rose said, "If you don't mind, I think I'd like to stay up here a while longer."

Chapter 23

AT THE FORT TILLMAN rail platform, Marcus Wales and Yelena quizzed the ticket master. Back at Kitty Hart, Boone Crowe had pressed a wad of folded currency from the recovered bank money into Wales' hand. *See to their needs*, Crowe had said. *It's been over three years since this money's been lost. Hell, they've probably gone bust by now anyway.* Wales wasn't sure he believed that, but he wasn't in a position to argue. Now, Yelena and Hazel, both in pretty new dresses and a suitcase full of others, tried to decide where they wanted to go.

"Well," the ticket master drawled, "there's Omaha. And St. Louie. Cincinnati."

"Any place smaller?" Yelena's life had begun in St. Louis. Too many disagreeable memories lurked there.

The ticket master studied his map. "Near a thousand on the way and beyond. There is Springfield, Illinois, though. President Lincoln resides there. In his crypt, of course."

"Have you ever been there?"

"I've been everywhere, ma'am."

Yelena looked at Marcus. "What do you think?"

"It's not up to me," he said. "Ask Hazel what she thinks."

"How does Springfield, Illinois, sound, honey?"

Hazel joined them at the ticket window. "I want to see Mister Lincoln."

The ticket master smiled. "He's dead, child. But his spirit is still mighty big in that town."

Wales paid for the tickets, and together they waited for the train. It rumbled up from the south, from Cheyenne, belching black smoke and bellowing its shrill whistle. Yelena turned to Marcus Wales, tears hanging from her lashes. "We owe you our lives, Marcus."

Wales said nothing, but touched her face with a gentle hand. They embraced briefly, and then the two girls boarded the train, the engine chuffing, and in a minute it was gone, winding through the flat, sagebrush country, heading east.

Cora saddled Stella and alone rode in the direction of the river Axel Harrington had spoken of. It was tree-lined and secluded. After dismounting, she drew her horse into the protection of the thickets and tied it to a low branch. The river was high from winter's melt-off, but she found a sandy approach and lingered there, studying the dark water throwing white crests around the river rocks.

After a while, making sure the place was uninhabited, she undressed and entered the water, moving toward a calm fjord. The water was cold, and she shivered nearly uncontrollably for a long time, suffering through its icy grip. Finally, she settled down, submerging herself up to her neck. Pun'ne had given her a bar of lavender soap, and she clutched it now, under the water. She stood then and lathered herself, the soft fragrance new to her and delighting her senses.

She washed in this manner repeatedly, as if trying to cleanse herself of deeper stains than simple trail dirt. She shampooed her hair with vigor, wishing, as she did this, that she could also purify her very mind as well, swabbing away unwanted memories. Finally, she stood, river water cascading off her in sheets, resembling sculptured statues of Venus and Aphrodite, their images reprinted in books.

Dressing then, she pushed Stella into a gallop across the high plains, away from the town. The wind beat her face, and mixed with the sun and the smell of sage and early flowers, Cora felt an exhilaration utterly strange to her. While standing in the river, she had watched the soap suds of her former self swirl and then race away down the river. With it had gone the strange attitudes of anger and defiance. In her seventeen years, they had gotten her nothing but heartache.

194

She rode now, pressing Stella to one final limit. Pulling up on the crest of a rise, she let her eyes pan the land, where the sloping plains of the territory sank and swelled like waves on the ocean. Here lay in geography, the very symbol of her denials. That life would be just as she wanted it to be, flat and smooth as a table-top. It was the ignorance of youth, she saw now. These rising and falling hills far better characterized life, and this new realization was a bitter thing to have to acknowledge. Her long attraction to Zebadiah Wilcox, she understood now, was because they both shared a similar meanness to those around them. Cora, in her mind only, had been right, all the time and in every decision— until suddenly she was wrong.

Before going back to the schoolhouse, she pulled her long hair over her shoulder and let the lavender fragrance fill her senses. For the first time in her life she wanted—needed—to find Rose and ask for her help. There was a past to put to rest. And a blurry future to ponder. Zebadiah Wilcox did not rescue her. He never could have, even had he lived.

Boone Crowe waited until dark to enter Fort Tillman, and even then he rode in from the backside, coming through the alley between the livery stable and one of the dozen saloons. He dis-mounted and led the horse through the open doors of the livery. It was his hope he would find the Ghost Horse stabled there, but after a search, he came up empty.

Next he rode quietly out toward the tent town. The one-armed preacher would know anything worth knowing about the Utah women and the rest. Most of the whores' tents were empty, having moved down to their assigned places in the saloons and gambling establishments. The usual mongrels put up a racket, barking to high heaven until Roman's pony put a hoof into one of their yapping jaws, sending it off with a whine and a whimper.

An orange glow illuminated the padre's tent, and Crowe

dismounted in front of it. His arm, still in its make-shift sling, seemed frozen from lack of movement. If he looked as haggard as he felt, he might put a fright in his friend.

"Padre?" he said. "You handy?"

The flap opened, and the one-armed preacher stared into the face of the marshal.

"Well, if it isn't Lazarus. Folks here have given you up to the coyotes." He pulled the flap wider and ushered Crowe in.

"Sit before you fall, Boone."

Coffee came next, and Crowe savored it hungrily. He listened to the preacher's banter. "Your boy made it here. With his pretty little colt, the girl who lost her leg."

"Roman's here?"

"Not here. I put them up for a couple of nights. They're both at Doc Wills' place now."

"Why Doc Wills?"

"Well, Boone. Craziest thing. Doc took a real shine to that boy's skill with a knife. Took him on as an apprentice."

"If you weren't a padre, I'd think you were lyin."

"Sure as rain, Boone. The boy didn't want to at first, but old Wills made him an offer he could not turn down."

"Which was…"

"'Give me a year,' Doc says. 'I need a young man with your skill,' he says. Even arranged for them both to live in the big house with him. And promised further to have a friend of his manufacture a special wooden leg for the girl."

Boone Crowe took this in, trying to put the words into a picture he could understand.

"Therefore, I performed a little operation of my own self. Those two were like a couple of doves about to bust every time they looked at each other. So I done my duty as a shepherd of the Lord. I married them up proper and tidy."

Finishing his coffee, Crowe felt exhaustion overtaking him. He looked at the one-armed preacher, past the lamp's glow and into his shadowed face. "Any news about the others?"

"Met your man, Wales. And his gabby-jawed partner, Rufus. But I did hear that some of them departed from here on the train a day or two back."

That's it then, Crowe thought.

"Why don't you stretch out on that cot there? I'll turn down this lamp, and you can get some rest. You look like badger bait."

"I'll probably snore."

"Can't be worse than cannon roar. And I withstood plenty of that."

Boone Crowe stood unsteadily, unhitched his spurs, and unbuckled his pistol belt. Then his big brimmed hat, rimmed with dust and sweat, fell beside it. With care he lifted the sling from over his head and dropped it onto the floor. It took him several minutes of maneuvering before he could get the tightness out of it. Finally, he lay down heavily on the canvas cot. "What'd Wales look like?"

The one-armed preacher spread a blanket over the marshal and sat back down on his stool.

"Ready and able."

Crowe turned on the cot. "Somethin got a hold of that boy. I sent him back home once. But he come back, hard as flint. Reckon he's still around?"

The one-armed preacher thought for a moment. "Well, I haven't seen him lately."

Even with eyes closed, Crowe said, "If he's still around in the morning...I might just pin a badge on him."

The two conspirators met in the lobby of the Saxon Hotel an hour before sunrise. Cigar smoke and black coffee. All that remained of a plate of early morning biscuits was crumbs. It was deceit in its most vile form, and each man relished in it. They viewed their wily plot as a mission of goodwill. A leading of the blind. A healing of the tormented. Both men present knew that the recoil could be heartbreaking, if not deadly.

Each had a part to play, acting on the flimsiest of evidence. They broke up their meeting just as the sun cut through the thin line of cottonwoods edging the east side of town. One of the conspirators rode away while the other man walked up the road and into the rising sun.

Marcus Wales knew where he was going. Earlier that morning he had left the marshal's Ghost Horse with the liveryman. He had brought Yelena's horse on a lead behind him. *Marshal Crowe will be around pretty soon, I reckon,* he'd said. *See that he gets this pale critter back. If he asks on me, tell him I'm long gone.*

He was back at the schoolhouse now collecting his few belongings. Bedroll, shotgun, two new shirts, a leather vest and spurs, all from the bank money. He pressed some bills into Axel's reluctant hand for the care of Rose of Sharon and Cora, whatever their needs might be. Wales had taken a bath and had a shave at the local bathhouse, and a new, green bandana ornamented his neck. His horse, previously Yelena's spotted paint, stood saddled in front of the schoolhouse, where he and Harrington bid each other farewell.

Throughout this leave-taking, Cora stood on the low porch watching him, her arm wrapped around one of the columns, her expression cut off by morning shadows. Once mounted, Wales turned, and taking notice of her, he nudged his horse alongside her.

"You're leaving," she said. It wasn't a question.

"I am." Wales found it difficult to look at her. "I thought it best if I leave on good terms. For what it's worth."

Cora stepped off the porch and put her hand on the horse's neck. She looked up at Wales with fetching eyes. "It's worth a lot to me, Marcus," she said, her voice a whisper.

The sound of his first name, a thing he'd never heard coming from her—she who had tormented him—was both peculiar and terrible in its sweetness.

"Where are you going?" she asked, her hand still on the horse's neck, steadily stroking.

"Not certain," he answered.

"Where's that?"

"North, maybe. I've never been there. I reckon you oughta know that. But it's the opposite direction of Utah."

Cora turned away suddenly and stepped back into the shadow of the porch.

Wales swung his horse around. "What about you?" he asked over his shoulder. But the girl didn't answer. She only shook her head. He tipped his hat to her, but he wasn't sure if she was even looking at him anymore, so he gently put a spur to the paint and rode out of the schoolyard and over the hill.

He rode a mile and stopped. After dismounting, he dropped the reins and stomped through the saw grass. He kicked at a clod of dirt and sent it flying into pieces. Utah, in his mind, was so far away it had practically disappeared. So if it had disappeared, then so should all that ever happened there. Wales picked a wild flower from the ground and examined the purple petals. He gazed across the wide, grand horizon, all the way to the shining mountains. In a moment of strange drama, he felt his throat tighten, realizing that out there, and beyond, lay his hard-fought freedom.

Had Wales possessed a mirror, he knew he'd not likely recognize his own image. A brief picture of the old Indian woman flashed before him. And the two devils who had harassed her, their bodies left for buzzard bait by his own hand. And then Frank King, a man he shot to protect a girl he hated. Wales looked at the flower and wondered if after all the killing, he still had a place for tenderness. He didn't want to lose everything about his old self. Boone Crowe, Wales had realized, for all his grit and fire, still showed a quietness of heart.

Wales walked to the paint and put his boot in the stirrup.

Then he swung himself back into the saddle. When he reentered the schoolyard, he saw that nothing had changed, Cora was still standing on the porch as she had been, and he could see that she was watching him approach. He rode directly up to her. The girl's eyes spoke for her, and Wales could see her wonder.

"Did you forget something?" she asked finally.

"I might have. It depends."

"Depends? On what?"

Wales turned his head in the direction of birdsong. He did not look at her when he said, "It depends on you." He was afraid to meet her eyes, afraid it would be the face he had grown up despising, the face of mockery.

"What are you asking?" Her hands were shaking so she clasped them together to help stop the tremors.

He finally did look, and he saw not mockery, rather atonement. He saw a face of needed clemency. He swallowed. "I reckon I wanna know just how far we've come. Have you and me come to where we don't have to look back?"

Her nod was birdlike, humble and fearful together.

Marcus Wales allowed himself a long gaze into the sky and land around him and then back to the girl. "There's a heap of loneliness out there, Cora." Her name sounded strange coming off his tongue. "In our own errors, we've added to that heap." Here his speech faltered, for he knew not which direction to take it. Finally, he said, "It doesn't seem likely that a few words can change all that."

Cora's eyes were downcast. A sudden fluttering of several yellow butterflies came off a wild rose bush gripping the porch rail and passed before her face, one perching on the top of her head. She started to reach up to brush it away when Wales said, "Don't."

She lowered her hand and looked at him, the butterfly, still alighted there, wings slowly batting. "What?" she said.

He stared at her. "When I ride away, this is the way I want to remember you. With a butterfly in your hair."

Horse and rider, as they grew smaller in the distance, seemed to Cora like a disappearing ship on a wide sea.

In the backroom of the undertaker's office, Boone Crowe looked hard at the four caskets leaning against the wall, and at the four pale-faced dead men who occupied them. It was his first concentrated inspection of the widow makers, and looking at them, he saw the same cruel aspect that he had seen in so many others he had hunted and killed. The young boy with curly hair was badly damaged, his shirt showing the three bullet holes from Cora's Colt.

He recognized Frank King, seeing him now up close. They had crossed paths several years ago. A gambler and plotter. The man had ridden away from a saloon shooting in Bradley some time back. Like most all of them, luck catches up. His belly showed two holes, and the pain of those wounds showed clearly in his countenance. Kammers was of the ilk Crowe hated deeply. A whelp, of a gentry's upbringing, his madness was probably a curse of incestuous inbreeding. A whole host of otherwise fine southern boys—some Crowe himself had killed—lay slaughtered in the fields because of the likes of Kammers' kind.

Crowe stopped in front of Smoot. The look of disbelief was still on the old Confederate general's face. The peculiar fellow who had finally shot him, the toothless Yankee Rufus Mead, must have seemed to Smoot, even as he was dying, as a cruel form of Civil War irony. Boone Crowe had no pity for any of them.

"I held them for ya, Marshal. Young fella said you'd be along to set things straight."

The marshal nodded at the undertaker. "Bury 'em where you bury all skunks."

On the boardwalk outside, Crowe saw Rufus sitting on a bench across the street. He motioned him over, and they went in the hotel lounge and had a beer and then sat discussing a long-ago war over cigars. He owed the old fighter something, having finished up the last of the ugly business at Kitty Hart. There would be no charges filed, not against him. Passing the gun to the girl Cora, and then sending Smoot to hell was pardon enough as far as Crowe was concerned.

Rufus talked of Gettysburg and then his captivity in Andersonville, and Boone told of his struggles in the Wilderness and later at Cold Harbor. There were other battles too, and both men found an absurd kind of pleasure in learning of the other's adventures in the twilight of twenty-years' distance. When Marshal Crowe finally saddled up the Ghost Horse, Rufus Mead did the same with the horse he'd taken as a prize from the dead Mr. Smoot. They rode out of Fort Tillman together, heading for Buffalo.

Chapter 24

THE SURPRISE SNOW STORMS and the spring rains finally gave way to the warmer days of late May. In the high country, there was bear grass, blooming powder white against the green aspens. Everywhere, across the plains, was Indian paintbrush and the yellow flowers of the prickly pear. Rivers and streams ran high and clear, and the spirited song of meadowlarks echoed through the grass. Cattle shared pastures with antelope and an occasional moose or deer. The town of Buffalo fell upon peaceful times.

At the far end of town came the persistent rhythm of hammers striking nails and the frequent scraping drag of a saw's blade clawing though wood. Planks were being laid out to make a floor big enough to dance on, and a roof, open on all sides, filling out the gazebo structure. A raised platform for a fiddle and banjo band was being erected by two local carpenters, and by nightfall of this day, there would be bunting and banners hanging from pillar to pillar.

Standing beside a wagonload of supplies, stood Hawken Canady, prosperous rancher from three hills over to the east. After a winter and spring of courting, Paige Canady had finally corralled her man, getting hitched in a private ceremony to the shy but durable deputy marshal Rud Lacrosse, the one-armed preacher presiding. The festivities that were to take place was old man Canady's wedding present to his only daughter. Tonight the town of Buffalo would light up the night with dancing, and a long line of young fellows wishing to kiss the bride would be relieved of a dollar for every kiss. Rud Lacrosse himself would arrest any violators.

Men and women worked side-by-side like ants, crowded at the elbows to get the last nail driven and the final wreaths of morning glory to grace the arbor entry. The day had been made to order, with sunshine aplenty and only an occasional cloud sailing the sky in what seemed like curiosity. By dusk the folks called it a grand achievement and a whole mite more cheerful than having to build a gallows. Tired, they went off to wash their sweaty bodies and dress for the party.

Boone Crowe sat in the barber's chair while Gust Schmidt clipped his locks. A shave, too, left his cheeks bare, leaving only chin whiskers and his customary sweeping mustache.

"You reckon Rud'll be any good as a deputy now? Being married and all?" Gust ventured.

"I told him he could quit if he wanted to. He jist gave me that look of his. Told me I oughtn't to try and run him off."

"Well, he's been steady all right." Gust clipped and then stopped again. "But that Paige is pretty as a peach blossom. If my wife looked like that I'd never cut another head of hair."

Crowe held back a laugh. "You're a damn liar, Gust. The whole town knows yer wife Ella is the handsomest woman in three counties. And a damn sight too pretty for the likes of you."

"I'll take that as a compliment. Unless you're planning on stealing her. Then I'll have to cut one of them ugly ears of yours off."

Boone Crowe did laugh now, but it wasn't a mirthful laugh. "I'm afraid I'm past the age of romance, Gust. So yer safe. And Ella is especially safe."

It was everything a town gathering should be. The braying of harmonicas and the sawing of fiddles floated across the pasture like a thing ordained. Two banjo pickers fought for harmonic superiority, while a barker called out the reels and waltzes. The two conspirators stood in separate corners of the vast gazebo, each acknowledging the others with a nod or a wink. The music continued, lively and festive, and the dancers swayed as if all worries and troubles had been checked at the gate.

These two held a collective eye on Boone Crowe, who came late and stood away from the crowd, his back against one of the columns. An assortment of townsfolk, making their rounds, stopped for a few minutes of conversation with the lawman. Judge Schaffer, uncommonly free of his usual pomposity, exchanged pleasantries as did Sheriff Clayton Murdock who moved among the crowd with an eye open for trouble. The tall, lean lawyer, Paul Lindekagel III, danced every dance with someone new each time.

At the agreed signal, the two conspirators meandered over and stood by Boone Crowe, drawing him into small talk. They stood like this for five full minutes, chatting about horses and weather, waiting for the fiddlers to stop. In the brief lull, the one-armed preacher complimented the marshal on his crisp white shirt and brushed Stetson. Harrington made a joke about Crowe's absence of spurs. Finally, the music started up again, a slow waltz, and the trap was set. Across the floor, moving toward them through the crowd, in a full length dress of meadow green, emerged Rose of Sharon.

Boone Crowe felt the claw of dread squeezing his heart. Rose stood before him, betraying nothing. Wales gave him an elbow. "I think she wants to dance, Marshal."

Crowe looked for an avenue of escape, his heart a pump, pushing and pulling his blood in a frenzy. He had not forgotten how beautiful she was, for her face had been in his mind every day. But here, and now, his knees nearly crumbled. He had not laid eyes on her since his discourteous sendoff at Kitty Hart.

"I ain't danced in a lifetime," he said, flushed, fear putting a sputter in his voice.

The one-armed preacher gave him a slight nudge, and Rose of Sharon held out her hand. Crowe looked from one to the other and then finally back to Rose. He was cornered. Tentatively, he took her hand and allowed himself to be lead into the crowd of dancers. He knew what he must do, and so he did it. Putting his arm around her waist, he began leading her, clumsily at first, his feet as fearful as the rest of him.

Leaning close so she could be heard, she asked about his wound.

"Fine," he said, biting off the word. Then managed to add, "Thanks to you."

They danced in silence for a full minute before Boone said, "I figured you went back to Utah."

"I could have. But I decided to wait."

"Wait for what?"

The music ended on a long chord, and they found themselves staring at each other. The whole crowd buzzed, and then the music struck up again, a squeezebox leading off. For an instant, Crowe remembered holding this woman close to him in the alley at Kitty Hart, and so, instinctively, he pulled her close again. This song was slower yet, and putting his face near to hers, he could smell her hair, its freshness. His terror mounted, piling higher, as if stone stacked on stone. It was worse than the men he had faced in battle. Or the men years ago, right here in Buffalo, when he stood in the street, facing three of them, waiting to be killed. Instead, he killed all three.

Whether proper or not, he realized that they were dancing so close he could feel her heartbeat against his own. *She's alive*, he thought. The realization nearly choked him. *She is alive, and Eva is dead.* He turned her in a circle, deathly afraid he would step on her, and as they danced, he glanced at the torches that burned outside the gazebo to brighten the festive surroundings. He stole a look at her face. Her eyes were closed, and he wished at that moment he might know the secrets of her heart.

When the music stopped again, Rose took Crowe's hand and led him down off the gazebo and into the dim shadows away from the torchlight. He followed her clumsily but obediently, knowing to resist would end everything, and he knew now he was not ready to be finished. They walked a long way up the street, the music and the clamor of the crowd growing fainter. In front of the Occidental Hotel they stopped. Rose sat down on a bench. She still had his hand, but he remained standing.

"I know how scared you are, Boone Crowe. I may be more scared than you." She made a gesture to release his hand, so he sat down next to her. He removed his Stetson and kneaded his fingers through his hair. "There's a lot of things I'd like to say," Rose said, "but I don't want to say them if it would be for nothing."

Boone considered this. "I'm a hard man. Maybe even a bad man. And sometimes I can be a clumsy, three-legged scarecrow. I know more about rustlers than I do about a woman's needs. I'm plum awkward as a fence post when I'm cornered by one."

"And you figure I've cornered you."

He finally found the courage to turn and face her. Rose's face shone radiant in the moonlight. "I'm likely to take up stuttering here in a minute."

She laughed, and her laugh was the most beautiful sound he'd ever heard.

"Boone Crowe, I know you've been hurt. It's written all over you. You're not good at hiding it."

Crowe said nothing.

Rose stared at the stars. "I know all about that kind of sadness. I see it every time I look in the mirror. I'm thirty-five years old. And all I have to show for it is what you see before you."

Impulsively, Crowe reached out and took hold of her hand again.

After a while she said, "I'm staying at Mrs. Taylor's Boarding House. I think I've had enough dancing for one night. Would you care to walk me home?"

He stood without speaking. The walk was short, and as they stood on the porch, the music playing softly in the distance, he fought with words too dangerous to speak. She touched his chest, where the bullet had torn through him. Her touch was gentle, and after everything else, it remained the one connection between them. "Good night, Boone Crowe."

The marshal ordered a whisky but never drank it. It sat on the bar top in front of him, its amber liquid reflecting the flame from a lamp. Leftover revelers from the dance had wandered into the saloon, but as night wore on, and after a few beers, even they moved on. By two in the morning, Boone Crowe was alone. He had moved from the bar to a table, his untouched whisky left behind. The bartender, polishing glasses with a towel, asked him if he wanted some breakfast, but Crowe shook his head.

"You look and act like you're drunk as a monkey, Marshal. But you ain't touched a drop all night."

"I need a clear head, Sam."

"You fixin to kill a man tomorrow?"

"If only it was that easy."

After another hour, Boone Crowe left the saloon and went to the livery and saddled up the Ghost Horse. He rode out of town into the darkness, and in another hour, he came to the little spread he was close to owning. He only owed another seventy-five dollars. It was to have been where he and Eva made a new start. But he didn't think about that now. Instead, he sat on the hill overlooking the little house, the barn, and the corrals. His old faithful horse, Hunter, was already boarded here, happy as a clam in sand with a whole pasture to himself.

The stars were bright, and here he could see all the way to the second layer of the heavens, stars so thick it was frightening. The fellow he was buying the place from had already moved out. An old gent with a daughter in Texas who plied for his company. After a while, he nudged the Ghost Horse down into the yard, and he saw Hunter lift his head and nicker. After dismounting, he walked to the corrals, and then back to the dark porch. A coyote took up its song where the trees crowded the hills, and Boone Crowe nearly surrendered to a foolish urge to howl back.

The one-armed preacher, the conniver. He and Harrington. They were in this together. But the padre. He'd have something to say. Some blasted words of wisdom that would stop Crowe short in his complaining tracks. Something like, *let the dead bury the dead.* The meaning of that being clear enough. Was he really dead, he wondered. He'd sure enough felt dead these past years. But now?

The Ghost Horse stood patiently, ears up as if waiting for an answer. "Stop looking at me that way." He peered through the window of the house, seeing nothing for the darkness. But he imagined light. He imagined a fire in the grate and a table with two chairs.

Boone Crowe stood for a long time before finally walking back to the horse and mounting. He rode as if he were young again, as if his body wasn't full of scars and busted pride. He rode without stopping until he reached the door of Mrs. Taylor's Boarding House on Third Street. It was five in the morning, but he pounded on the door until Mrs. Taylor opened up, still in her bedclothes.

"Marshal, have you lost your mind?"

"Maybe." He tried to look over the woman's shoulder. "I need to see Rose."

"For land's sake. She's still in bed. Are you here to arrest her?"

"I will if I have to."

"Oh, gracious. Well, sit down on the steps then and wait." She left, shaking her head.

He did as instructed, suddenly realizing he was half naked without his Colt or his spurs, the worst kind of helplessness. After a time, he heard the door open behind him. He stood and saw before him a living princess. The sun, only barely up, cast such a radiance on her face Crowe fairly gasped.

"You're an early caller, Marshal."

Crowe was too intent on the business at hand that he feared any pause in the action might scare him off. "Rose of Sharon," he said and then said it again. "Rose of Sharon, I apologize for never having spoken it out fully before now. It's a name fitting a lady pretty as you."

"Why, Boone Crowe, you make me blush." And she did.

He put his hands in his pockets so he wouldn't wave his arms around like a goose. "You've been the cause of many a sleepless night, Rose. Including this one. And so…I must get to the point quick before I lose my nerve." He looked at the ground momentarily and then gazed straight into her face. "Rose, I'm plum stupid about things like this. I don't even know how I come to be standing here. But…" he took a step closer to her, "I near beat myself senseless. Every since that day at Kitty Hart. When… when I put my arms around you. There in the alley. And I've felt you in my arms every day since. So…if you're willin. I…I reckon I'm askin for yer hand. But if yer answer is—"

Stepping close, Rose put her fingers to his lips to hush him up. Tears were gathering in her eyes now, so with her other hand, she made a hasty swipe at her cheek. "That was a fine speech, Boone Crowe. And my answer is yes." She closed her eyes for a brief moment. "I would have said yes back at Kitty Hart."

Chapter 25

Judge Schaffer paced the creaky floor of his chambers waiting for the marshal to show his face. A man named Cecil Borrows had just shot up a saloon in the backwater town of Pledge and rode off on somebody else's horse. Pledge residents hinted that Borrows might be linked to some local rustling too. He heard the courthouse door open and boot heels in the hall.

Marshal Rud Lacrosse entered the judge's chambers, seeing Schaffer's spectacles reflecting lamplight. He sat down in a chair without invitation and crossed his legs. The judge waved a yellow telegram message in the air. Lacrosse snatched it from his hand and read it.

"Take Deputy Wales with you. If it's rustlers, it'll take both of you." Marshal Lacrosse left the judge's chambers without saying a single word. It was always better that way.

Marcus Wales had finally made it to Buffalo after his long ride to the North Country. Once, after being deputized by the new marshal, Rud Lacrosse, he passed back through Fort Tillman on lawing business, and with the hope of Cora still being there. He found her working behind the counter of a shipping and freight establishment, the shop heavy with the scent of saddle leather and sawdust. They exchanged pleasantries, her eyes taking in the badge pinned to his linen shirt-front. His poise, a thing now of settled sand, allowed him to speak frankly to her, about places he had seen in Idaho and Canada. Lonesome places, he told her, where the stars and the mountains were his only company. His words revealed the slow drag of confidence.

Even in the dimly lit freight office Cora could see the sparkle in Marcus Wales' eyes. They shone with a strange blend of certainty and caution, born out of miles and months of lonely soul searching. It seemed cast there like ivory and she nearly shuddered at the sight of its beauty.

Wales removed his hat and brushed back his hair with his

fingers. "Axel told me where you were. So I got it in my head to pay you a visit."

Cora felt a tightening in her throat. A tightening all over. "When did you get that in your head?" Her voice was light as air.

Marcus Wales blushed. "'Bout a month ago."

She tried to hide a giddy laugh, but it came out like sparrow-song.

Turning toward the door he'd left open when he entered, Wales stared out at the street. "I didn't come here to waste my words, Cora." He turned back to her. "At the risk of sounding like a fool, I left that door hanging wide, hoping we might walk through it together."

She took in the full of him, standing there in his lawman chivalry.

"Unless, of course, you're tied down to job or man," he added.

Cora had never been one for crying. But if this wasn't a moment for it, she feared she'd never know another.

Boone Crowe had exceeded his stock. It had always been his dream to have ten cows, but he had added an eleventh as a present to Rose. It was a little, pretty, black heifer calf that danced around the pasture like a circus clown. In the mornings, Boone and Rose sat on the porch with coffee, watching the critter hop around. Later they would ride the fifty acres, Rose on Hunter and Boone on the Ghost Horse. In the evenings, they would sit at the kitchen table, facing each other over steak and potatoes, Boone's favorite. Then back out to the porch to listen to the whippoor-wills and mourning doves.

"The postmaster gave me a letter yesterday when I was in town. It was addressed only to Rose of Sharon, Buffalo. Hoping I would be here, I guess."

"Whose it from?"

"It's from Yelena. Springfield, Illinois, the postmark said. Illinois of all places. She said Hazel is fine and in school there. But the big news is that she met a man who builds houses. Says the town is growing, so he is very busy. His name is Moses, and her letter went on about how handsome he is. Girl stuff. Anyway, Hazel has grown near a foot she said, and the house they live in is just down the street from where Mr. Lincoln lived when he was still a lawyer."

The mention of Lincoln set a spark in Crowe. He'd seen the great man once. It was at Petersburg, after the battle, and he was riding a horse through the smoking ruins of buildings and men.

"Yelena said the train ride was fine. Better than the one she came out west on."

Boone nodded. "Makes me think." He had his feet up on the porch railing. "A fella named Tugs Bigelow and I took a train ride out to the ocean once. Place called Astoria. Have you ever seen the ocean, Rose?"

"No, I have not." Her smile betrayed her curiosity.

"I was thinking maybe September. The oceans as big as the sky at night. We could walk on one of those piers where the boats haul in salmon. Tuna and the like. We could go on a boat ride ourselves. Why, Bigelow said they have boats that'll take a person all the way to Alaska."

Rose of Sharon took hold of his hand. The summer moon was full, and it climbed above the hills and the trees, putting down a path of silver light.

It was winter and Buffalo, New York, was buried in snow. It was always buried in snow in winter, and ice on the Niagara River seemed to bunch up on the shore before spilling over the falls. The carriage dropped the man off in front of the hotel, but he didn't go inside. Instead, he turned up his fur collar and stood under the street's lamplight. It was not the first night he had done this, but it would be the last.

Half an hour later a man in similar attire, dressed for the cold, stepped out of the hotel lobby and onto the boardwalk. He stood for a few minutes watching the gray sky. It was almost midnight, and his pockets were full of winnings from poker. Taking a cigar from a breast pocket, he lit it, the flare of the match exposing his face.

When he stepped into the street, the man from the carriage approached him. He wasted no time. "Othello Hardy."

The gambler stiffened. "Who are you?"

The man from the shadows only repeated the name. "Othello Hardy."

"I don't use that name anymore."

The Colt roared, filling the quiet night with thunder and flame. Othello Hardy lay on his back, his red blood spreading in the white snow. Men from the hotel poured out of the lobby like ants, looking right and left. Two men saw the body, and they rushed to it. They stared at him, realizing it was the man who only moments ago had been at their gambling table.

"What's that," one of them said.

They looked close. On the dead man's forehead rested a star. A deputy's badge, one of the star's prongs slightly bent.

ACKNOWLEDGEMENTS

In *The Widow Makers*, the fifth in the Marshal Boone Crowe series, I owe a debt of gratitude to Jennifer Moorman, to whom this novel is dedicated. An original version of this novel was lost a decade ago when a hard drive in my computer was fried beyond retrieval. And so it became a ghost that haunted my muse for years after. It was the love for the character Boone Crowe, which Jennifer expressed over the first four novels that gave me the courage to resurrect the lost story and rewrite it into what it is before you now. Had Jennifer not shown her affection for the old marshal, there would never have been this revived, and better, edition of *The Widow Makers*.

It is my wife, Rebecca's relished duty to pour over my first proof-copy with her yellow highlighter that—though setting my teeth on edge—finds those errors that I have missed. Opening the pages of this proof is her first view of each novel, and they are better for her efforts.

Rachel Boruff, of Rachel Thornton Photography, gets credit for all the Boone Crowe book covers, front and back. Watching her work with eased skill with her camera and her talent for pulling in the natural surroundings to compliment her subjects is an inspiring thing to witness. My thanks to her.
There are characters in this story, inspired—with their consent—by real people who I need not mention by name, as they will know who they are from the opening paragraph. My thanks to them. And an added thanks to Kymberlee Nicole Gimmaka who helped form the complex character of Cora. It was this inspiration, at times, that helped carry the story.

Humility is a virtue, pride is not. To whatever end my writing takes me, it began and remains a gift from God.

Buck Edwards finds kinship with the windblown tumbleweeds of America's prairies and wide open spaces. A traveling man, Edwards, when not rooted between the pages of a good book, can be found tramping the historical sites across the country, from Fort Ticonderoga and Plimoth Plantation, to Gettysburg, Fort Sumter, and the Alamo.

His western writing-roots came from a youthful love for the books of Zane Grey, Owen Wister, Alan Lemay, and Conrad Richter. Raised around horses and cattle, Edwards enjoys studying the landscape surrounding his prairie home in eastern Washington, as well as the regions where his books take place—Wyoming, Nevada, Utah, and Montana.

When asked if Marshal Boone Crowe is his alter ego, Edwards refers them to writer Norman Mailer, who once explained that writers must be able to create characters that are stronger than they are, braver than they are, and perhaps even handsomer than they are. Edwards says that Marshal Boone Crowe is all of these things.

The *Marshal Boone Crowe* series consists of *Dead Woman Creek*; *Showdown in the Bear Grass*; *Judgment at Rattlesnake Wash*; *Track of the Wolf*; and *The Widow Makers*. A sixth installment to these westerns, *Shoot-out at Lost River*, is due out in 2016. They are all available through Amazon in paperback, or on Kindle, and also on Barnes and Noble's NOOK.

Made in the USA
Middletown, DE
21 August 2019